THE ARIZONA KID

When former hired gun Calvin Taylor took the job of sheriff of Oxford County, New Mexico, it was for one reason only — to catch, or kill, the notorious Arizona Kid, and pick up the fifteen hundred dollars reward the governor had secretly offered. Taylor found himself on the trail of the infamous gang known as the Regulators, hunting down a man who'd once been his friend. The pursuit came, in every sense, a journey of death.

ANDREW McBRIDE

THE ARIZONA KID

Complete and Unabridged

LINFORD
Leicester

First published in Great Britain in 1998 by
Robert Hale Limited
London

First Linford Edition
published 1999
by arrangement with
Robert Hale Limited
London

British Library CIP Data

McBride, Andrew
   The Arizona Kid.—Large print ed.—
Linford western library
1. Western stories
2. Large type books
I. Title
823.9'14 [F]

ISBN 0–7089–5497–9

Published by
F. A. Thorpe (Publishing) Ltd.
Anstey, Leicestershire

Set by Words & Graphics Ltd.
Anstey, Leicestershire
Printed and bound in Great Britain by
T. J. International Ltd., Padstow, Cornwall

This book is printed on acid-free paper

Time to thank Michael Andrew; also Messrs Penn, Utley, Metz, Steckmesser, Upson and Garrett.

1

Calvin Taylor waited for the Arizona Kid.

He was waiting on the flat top of a mesa that reared a few hundred feet above the surrounding desert. He was sweating. He smelled fear in his sweat. Not surprising, given that he was waiting on a killer. He lifted his arms and saw his wrists were trembling slightly.

Was he getting soft? Were his nerves going? If so, he was a dead man, going up against Nino, the Kid.

Out loud he told himself, 'You've not gone soft, Taylor.' He hoped he'd convinced himself. After all he was long seasoned and tested in the fire; ten years in this dangerous trade, first as a scout against the Apaches, then as a range detective, a hired gun. A man with a reputation — a mankiller.

He was crouched under a white oak tree, at the edge of a little fire burning the ends of mesquite wands and raising the merest thread of smoke. He reached towards the spider over the fire, glimpsing his face reflected in the dull metal of the coffee pot. Skin weathered brown as an Indian's, hair moustache and new beard dark, but eyes blue as ice: women seemed to like that combination. A handsome man, but his face had grown hard with too much sun and weather and the tension that was always inside him. Even before he'd grown this beard, he'd looked older than his twenty-eight years.

Turning his head in any direction, Taylor could view the same bleak landscape: mountains, desert, south-eastern New Mexico Territory. Off south was the Mescalero Apache reservation. The Mescaleros had once terrorized this land. Now, in 1881, they were pretty much a beaten people, although a white eye should still watch out for himself, travelling alone through their country.

To the south-west, land gleamed silver in the westering sun. Down there were the White Sands, miles of salt desert. On the surface of the White Sands, Taylor had glimpsed a horseman's dust: the Arizona Kid's dust.

As he poured coffee into a tin cup, Taylor kept his eye on his lineback dun horse. When it lifted its fine head and stared off to the east, Taylor gripped with his left hand the fifteen-shot Winchester slanting against a rock beside him. He rested the carbine across his knees. The Kid was due to meet him alone, that was the deal: but what if he showed up with half a dozen of his friends instead?

Taylor's back was covered by the thick body of the oak, a scatter of rocks giving cover in front of him, and beyond that was open ground with a good field of fire. Open ground behind him too, where he couldn't be sneaked up on. He wore a Colt pistol, butt forward on his left hip, he had a spare pistol in his saddle-roll, a knife in his boot and enough ammunition to fight off a small army. He ought to feel safe, but . . .

The thing was the Kid moved so damn quiet, like a cat; he ought to have been an Apache he was so soft-footed. It was said he'd stolen horses out of Mescalero camps and Taylor could believe it. On top of that there was the damn wind . . .

The wind moaned blearily on the desert below, rippling surf waves of dust, thrashing the arms of the few stooped junipers that edged this plateau. The fox ears of the dun slanted eastward. Taylor glanced that way, his grip on the Winchester tightening, but couldn't see anything, just the trees flailing before the wind . . . and then there he was. Standing there as if he'd just dropped from the sky.

Taylor said, 'You take molasses in your coffee, as I recall.' He tried to hide the fear in his voice; he knew the Kid would see the tension in his face, however hard he tried to think it away.

The Kid approached. He was dressed pretty much Mexican, with a striped serape over his shoulders and a wide-brimmed Chihahueno hat shading his face, tied with a buckskin thong under the chin. He wasn't carrying a rifle or wearing a belt-gun as far as Taylor could see.

He halted and nodded towards the carbine in Taylor's hand. 'You don't need that, Taylor. I'm not heeled.'

'It's all right, Kid.' Taylor poured coffee for the two of them. 'It ain't pointed at you.'

The Kid smiled. He crouched down on the other side of the fire and took the cup Taylor offered him — with his *left* hand. His shooting hand dawdled on his knee. Taylor realized he was looking for the bulge in the Kid's sleeve or under the folds of the serape that meant a hideout gun and was

5

surprised at himself, because a hideout gun wasn't the Kid's style at all.

Around them the wind ebbed; they wouldn't need to shout through it. Nino drank his coffee like a thirsty man. 'I hear you got a new job, Taylor.'

'That's right.'

'But here in Oxford County?'

'I like it round here.'

The Kid gave his famous grin, showing his buck teeth. You might think those two splayed upper front teeth would spoil his looks, but instead they gave the Kid's face a jaunty friendliness, like a playful terrier. 'Well, I don't see no problems. You need me, Taylor. If it wasn't for us Regulators, you wouldn't have nothing to do.'

'Still calling yourselves 'Regulators', huh?'

'I suppose your new employers call us something else.'

Taylor nodded. 'That's right. They call you stock thieves.'

The Kid studied Taylor's face. His

6

grin winked out, an instant, before appearing again, a little less easy this time. Taylor went on, 'And they call you, Kid, a murderer.'

The Kid blinked. 'I never murdered anybody.'

'Zar Kelly — '

The other man sneered. 'That back-shooting, four-flushing . . . if any sonofabitch ever needed killing, it was him.'

'Sure. Kelly was rotten, venal, corrupt, a bribe-taker, pimp and murderer. He was also the county sheriff.'

'I don't make a habit of killing lawmen.'

'Glad to hear it.' Taylor smiled. 'Seeing as *I'm* county sheriff now.'

The Kid shook his head. 'I still don't figure why you took that job.'

'You know how I'm fixed. Living with Pilar. Nice and easy all the time . . . but I guess I'm not cut out to live Mexican. I need to be doing something.'

The Kid scraped dust from his

forehead with the back of his wrist. Salt dust covered him like hoar frost. Underneath, he had fair skin that burned easily, and medium brown hair; he was attempting to grow a moustache with his usual lack of success. Apart from his prominent teeth his most noticeable features were his green eyes. Nobody would have called the Kid, with his short nose, buck teeth and wisp of moustache, handsome, but the local *señoritas* didn't seem to mind, won over by his boyish, easy-laughing ways, his cat-green eyes. A slightly built young man, a little below middle height. Despite his nickname, the Kid looked to be about twenty-four or twenty-five; his real name was Henry McCarthy.

Nino said, 'We don't need to crowd each other. This is a big county. You could lose some eastern states in it.'

'Getting crowded for you.'

Nino was still grinning, although the grin was starting to look a little fixed now. For the first time Taylor thought the Kid looked tired. He was sweating badly. Maybe he was as tense as Taylor himself. Nino said, 'Maybe I'll try over in Texas.'

'Wouldn't, if I were you. Those ranchers over in the Panhandle, they're plenty sore at you, all the cattle and horses you've stole. They've upped the bounty on your head.'

The Kid's grin vanished. For a moment, as he glared at Taylor, he wasn't the laughing boy charming the *señoritas*, the happy-go-lucky cowboy who made friends easily; he was the Arizona Kid, wanted, or implicated in, half-a-dozen murders.

'I know why you took this job. All that horseshit about how you couldn't live Mexican. Truth is, you don't like living *poor*. You took the job for one reason only: money. And the real money is *me*. I've heard about it. How the governor's secretly raised the reward on me from five hundred dollars to fifteen hundred: that's what you'll get if you bring me in. Or kill me. That's the truth, isn't it?'

9

'If it is . . . maybe you should be flattered.'

Nino stood, his hands at his sides, poised like he was going to reach for a weapon . . . if he had one. 'That's all I am to you. A bounty. Like I'm some kind of animal to be hunted.'

Taylor drank coffee a moment, then said, 'This is a big country, Kid. Oxford County's only a little bit of it. You could always go back to Arizona. Or . . . '

'Like you said: I like it around here.'

Taylor sighed. He flung the grounds from his cup to the earth. 'That's it, then.'

Nino started to turn away, then halted, as if he'd remembered one more thing. He said, 'I figured we was friends, Taylor.'

Taylor thought he heard real hurt in the Kid's voice, almost a child's hurt: the pain of trust betrayed. Taylor began to shape a cigarette. He said, 'I like you, Kid. We've had some fun

10

times. But you ain't my friend. Never have been.' He let that sink in, then he added, 'And with fifteen hundred dollars on your head you might find even your *real* friends getting scarce.'

That brought a silence. The Kid said, 'Maybe you ought to settle it right now while you have the chance. Might save us both a lot of grief.'

'Maybe.'

The Kid stood a moment more, waiting for Taylor to kill him. When the lawman didn't move Nino turned away and began to descend the slope on the east face of the mesa. Taylor sat and smoked his cigarette, letting tension ease out of him. He was still a little bit afraid. And tired. He and the Kid were in about the same shape, he thought: worn down to the ends of their nerves. He felt something else, too: a curious sense of sadness, as if he'd just lost something important.

He stood and moved towards his horse. It was perhaps a hour to sunset. He had a long ride ahead of him, north to Agua Frio. He wanted to be through Dog Canyon before dusk; that was no place to be in darkness.

* * *

There were three of them waiting in Dog Canyon. They were in the cover of boulders on the slopes on both sides of the canyon, where they could take the man they were after in a triangular ambush. As the sun sank in the west and the shadows lengthened on the canyon floor, they checked their rifles, their handguns, their ammunition. They were taking no chances; they couldn't afford to, even with three-to-one odds. After all, they were going up against a notorious assassin: a shootist, a mankiller. They were going up against Calvin Taylor.

2

Just outside rifle shot of the entrance to Dog Canyon, Taylor reined in his horse. He studied the black jaws of the pass. A place with a grim reputation; from the Apache Wars and since, a good place for an ambush. Maybe that was why the Kid had come to the meeting unarmed: why take on Taylor face to face when some of his compadres could bushwhack him later? Make sure the new sheriff never collected on that $1,500. There'd still be enough shooting light in Dog Canyon to get the job done.

But going around the pass would put hours on to Taylor's journey and, anyway, the canyon might be empty, a place of shadow and ghosts.

He rode into the canyon. There was an eerie quiet in the place that gnawed at his guts, and a brooding quality in the shadows under the canyon walls, but he decided that was imagination too. He tried to think of something else. He thought about Pilar waiting for him in Agua Frio and his thoughts came back to the Kid and he wondered which one of them was the steadiest, the least nerve-worn, because that one would walk away from this. Taylor gazed at the ground ahead of him, studying the rocks and shadows on the slopes under the canyon walls, seeing nothing amiss. Then he felt the hairs prickle on the back of his neck and arms; it was only instinct, but it told him *that his enemies were behind him. His back felt wide as a barn door.* He turned in the saddle and the shot came.

The bullet whined past his ear.

His instinct had been right, the shot had come from behind. He glimpsed over his right shoulder, a dark wisp of powdersmoke!

Taylor yelled. A yell with a lot of fear in it. He spurred the dun and ducked low as the horse broke into a run.

Another rifle cracked. Off the slope above him, to the left. His instinct had only been half right, he was caught in a crossfire!

Taylor veered his dun up the slope, going at the rifleman there head on. The man fired again, missing again, by which time Taylor had worked his Winchester free of the saddle scabbard, laying the carbine across his arm, firing in reply. Then he swung one leg over the saddle and came down on the near side of the dun, landing on a slope of sand that shifted under him, almost went sprawling, then lunged upslope; almost running head on into a third man who reared from behind a boulder, a rifle in his hands. Taylor glimpsed the man's startled face, mouth wide to yell. He barely had time to swing his rifle about before Taylor was on him. He fired and Taylor felt the bullet snatch at his shirt front; then Taylor drove the barrel of his Winchester into the man's stomach and the other doubled forward. Taylor followed through with the riflebutt, catching his enemy alongside the jaw and spinning him backwards. Then Taylor was past him, running upslope.

There was another shot from behind him, then the man ahead yelled, 'Vincente!' A man in a red shirt lifted to fire. Taylor plunged down behind a circle of boulders, scrambling up to fire himself, looking for a target, but his enemy was back in cover.

The sheriff found he was gasping for air. He was pouring sweat and his arms shook quite violently; he was dizzy too. He tried to slow his breathing and get his trembling arms under control. After a time he decided he hadn't been hit. When he inspected his shirt he saw a ragged hole where a button had been whisked away. He said, 'Christ!' And then firing started again, from above and from the other side of the canyon.

Taylor decided there was no point trying to shoot two ways at once. He'd ignore the man behind him, unless he made a move across the canyon floor, concentrate on redshirt, the man ahead. Redshirt tried a couple of wide shots and then Taylor realized he was trying to angle richochets into his enemy's hiding place. Well, two could play at that game. There was a flat-faced boulder on the slope above redshirt's place of concealment. Taylor calculated angles and trajectories a moment. He fired at the boulder and heard the yowl of the richochet. He repeated the shot and redshirt yelled. He sprang upright, one hand behind him, pressed to his back. Taylor shot him. The man fell clear of the rocks, struck the slope and started to roll. Taylor shot him again and the body fetched up in a tangle of shale and brush, jackknifed around a small boulder. The rifle in his hand skittered downslope.

Taylor's arms started shaking again; he spent a minute getting himself back under control. While that was happening, he heard hoofbeats; the surviving ambusher making his way out of the canyon. The hoofbeats faded into silence.

Taylor could see the man he'd shot clearly, his red shirt now a darker colour, not much left of his face because a bullet had wiped it away, leaving just a bloody maw. Taylor stared at the dead man, feeling angry, then sick, then nothing. He studied the ground below him, looking for the man he'd felled with the riflebutt, not seeing him. Then there was a groan. Taylor trained his rifle on the sound; a man sat up, jerking up out of the shadow.

Taylor walked over to him, halted, keeping the rifle pointing at the man's chest. A young Mexican in nondescript clothing, shaking the dizziness out of his head. His mouth, chin and shirtfront were bloody, Taylor had maybe knocked out some teeth with the riflebutt. Taylor recognized him.

'Vincente Chavez.'

He was shocked. Vincente was a friendly kid he knew from Agua Frio;

Taylor had liked him. Liked him *and* his brother.

Taylor scooped up Vincente's rifle. In Spanish he asked the Mexican boy, 'Who was the other one, Vincente? The one run out on you?'

Vincente was feeling in his mouth, trying to stem the flow of blood; then he stared. 'Quirino — '

Taylor gestured upslope. Vincente turned his head slowly. When he saw the body snagged around the rock, he gave a cry of pain.

Taylor told him, 'Your brother's dead, Vincente.'

The prisoner hung his head a moment, then he glared at the lawman in hatred. Tears had already started in his eyes. 'Butcher!'

'What you expect? You and Quirino was lyin' up to butcher me. Get rid of any other weapons you got.'

'Not got any.'

'Get up.'

Vincente pushed himself off the ground. As he did so, he whipped

19

a long-bladed knife from his boot and made a cut at Taylor's ribs. Taylor was ready for that; he cracked Vincente across the forearm with the barrel of the carbine and saw the knife spill from his hand. For good measure, Taylor hit Vincente in the stomach with the butt of the carbine. Vincente folded forward, sinking to his knees with his arms wrapped around his belly.

Taylor waited until Vincente got some air back inside him. He asked, 'Who put you up to this? Was it the Kid?' When Vincente didn't answer, Taylor said, 'You damn fool!'

★ ★ ★

Taylor rode through Dog Canyon, Vincente going ahead of him, tied to his horse, Quirino following, tied head down over his. Beyond the canyon, Taylor found a place to roost where he couldn't be easily jumped, and cat-napped through the night. Vincente spent an even more

20

uncomfortable night in the same place, bound hand and foot. In the morning, the sheriff ate a frugal breakfast and fed his prisoner the same. When dust showed on the northern horizon he kicked out his breakfast fire and took his prisoner into the cover of high ground overlooking the trail. He waited with his Winchester in his hand.

Vincente said, 'My friends, coming. They'll make you bleat before you die, *gringo*.'

Taylor was a little shocked by the word, the traditional Mexican insult for Anglos. He thought he'd been accepted by the Mexicans here, but then he'd thought, also, that Vincente had been his friend. He shaded his eyes, watching the nearing dust. 'You're out of luck.'

'Uh?'

'Those are my friends, not yours.'

Vincente made a sound of disappointment. Taylor stood out in the open, where he could be clearly seen. Four horsebackers drew rein in dust before him. Four Anglos: the

Yerby brothers, and an Irishman, Pat O'Keefe.

The eldest Yerby — Zeke — shifted his considerable bulk in the saddle. 'What happened?'

Taylor told him. Zeke said, 'We're chasing horsethieves. Looks like those damn Regulators again.'

The next eldest brother — they called him Tiger Sam — stroked his right cheek where a deep scar cleft it from the corner of his eye to his mouth. Sam's eyes moved to Vincente. 'I see you kept one of them greasers alive. Why? Might as well kill him right now.'

Taylor said, 'Step down and help yourself to coffee, boys.'

As the riders dismounted, Vincente gave the sheriff a frightened look. 'These are your friends, Taylor? Your deputies? Those Yerbys — they're animals.'

Taylor sighed. 'I've got to take whatever help offers itself. I've got no choice. I can't do this job on my own.'

22

Pat o'Keefe and the youngest Yerby — Mose — approached. O'Keefe was a balding man in his thirties with a serious face, accentuated by his handlebar moustache. He was very tall, six four perhaps, and thin as a lath. Mexicans called him 'Juan Largo' or 'Long John'. As he studied Taylor's prisoner, he frowned.

'I never took you for a bushwhacker, Vincente. I always thought you was a good kid. Now look what's happened.' He shook his head sorrowfully.

Vincente said, 'Go to hell, Lengthy.'

Mose Yerby kicked Vincente in the shin. 'Watch your mouth around a white man.' He turned his quirt in his hands. 'Want a taste of this leather, peppergut?' He kicked the boy again, harder.

O'Keefe said, 'Enough of that, now.'

Mose turned. He glared at O'Keefe. 'What, Irish?'

Taylor said, 'Leave the boy alone.'

Mose raised his eyebrows. 'After he tried to put a bullet in you?'

'That's right.'

Mose spent a minute thinking about that. 'Sure, Sheriff.' He smiled. 'I was forgetting how you feel about Mexicans.'

There was another pause. Taylor realized Mose was waiting for him to do something, or say something, O'Keefe too. When Taylor didn't react, something happened to Mose's smile, a little contempt came into it. He moved away.

Taylor watched Mose walk over to his brothers. Once Taylor thought, he'd have answered Mose all right — with the gun in his belt. Maybe he was getting a bit of maturity, learning some restraint, the value of human life. Or maybe he was just going soft. He felt the dull tin of the six-pointed star on the left side of his shirt. Maybe taking on this job had been a bad mistake. He thought of Quirino, whom he'd liked and killed, of Vincente, whom he'd liked and who'd tried to kill him, of the Kid whom he'd liked and was now hunting like an animal. Then there were the Yerbys, whom he'd be happy to kill, only now they wore the same badges he did. And what about Paco and Pilar, how would they fit into this?

He came out of his reverie to see O'Keefe studying him, frowning. Taylor started to roll a cigarette. 'You boys take these Chaveses back to Oxford. Make sure the coroner has a chance to look over Quirino before you plant him. I'm going to Agua Frio.'

The Yerby brothers were laughing about something. The eldest and youngest Yerbys were a match in ugliness, Taylor thought. Both had bullet heads and a scant crop of brownish hair, almost lipless gashes for mouths, small, malevolent eyes. Their noses were narrow blades that hooked from moon faces. Mose had a no-neck stockiness; Zeke ten years older, had acquired a full sprawling belly. In contrast, the middle brother, Sam, was still fairly slim, a handsome man, or at least he had been until the Kid had taken a knife to his cheek.

O'Keefe gazed at the brothers, too. He said, 'They say the Yerbys were horsethieves themselves, over in Texas, or Arkansas, or wherever they come from.'

Taylor shrugged. 'Someone's past is their own business.'

'Hill-country trash.'

'Maybe, but they ain't short of guts. They don't run for the next county when the bullets start flying. That's the kind of men I need back of me.' He smiled grimly. 'Leastways, until I can get some better.'

Vincente asked, 'You gonna leave me with them?'

'They're taking you to Oxford.'

'Them Yerbys — they don't like Mexicans. They take me, I'll never get to Oxford. They'll kill me.'

'Yesterday you was trying to kill *me*.'

Taylor moved off some distance; O'Keefe came and stood alongside him. Taylor said, 'Try and keep the Yerbys from murdering Vincente.'

'If they want to kill him, they'll have to kill me first.'

The laughter from the Yerbys increased. They glanced over at the sheriff and paused, then laughed some more. Taylor felt a flicker of anger. He judged they were laughing at him and wondered, once again, why he hadn't pulled his gun on Mose. If it wasn't for the tin badge on his shirt . . . He told the Irishman, 'That's just what they will do, Pat.'

3

New Mexico had been part of the United States for a couple of generations, but you wouldn't think so looking at Agua Frio. Thus far only a handful of Anglo residents had found their way into the little settlement — Calvin Taylor was one. The rest of the populace were predominantly Mexican, people eking out a meagre existence from the crops they raised in irrigated fields, or the cattle they herded, or the sheep they grazed on the surrounding flats. Agua Frio itself was a scatter of low, flat-roofed adobes grouped around a plaza, with people sitting in the shade of their doorways, or moving out on the streets, making their way past mule-riders and horsebackers, past high-sided carts hauled by tiny oxen, cart wheels discs of solid wood screaming for grease, past pigs and chickens rooting in the potholes and wheel-ruts of the road.

Taylor rode into Agua Frio towards dusk, left his horse at the livery and walked over to the Garcia house. He was, he realized, expecting trouble, tensed and ready for it. But no onlooker glared at him; no one stepped in his way. Perhaps word of the doings in Dog Canyon hadn't reached this place yet . . .

He paused once crossing the street. Something wasn't right. Slowly, he realized what he'd expected to see or hear: festivities going on. There would be in other settlements, because today was the Fourth of July. But Agua Frio wasn't celebrating Yankee independence; in its heart and mind it was still part of Mexico.

When he entered the house, Pilar didn't ask him where he'd been, or what he'd done, but it hurt him, seeing the fear and tension in her face. She knew how it was with him now; every time he walked out of the door, he might not come back. And today, she'd have other reasons to be afraid. She'd be thinking of her husband, Miguel Garcia.

Two years ago today, 4 July 1879, three young Anglos, drifting cowhands, had come into Agua Frio. They were three-parts drunk already, but managed to get hold of some more liquor. As the drink took hold, they noticed that no one else in the village seemed to be celebrating Independence Day. They decided these local greasers weren't showing either white men like themselves, or the United States in general, quite enough respect. Their talk turned to Santa Anna and the Mexican War, to the slaughter at the Alamo and the Goliad massacre, bloody doings that happened long before they were born. One of them decided it'd be fun to make a spic on the street in front of them dance and fired at his feet. Then another decided he'd shoot off this beaneater's hat and fired; but his aim was off. His shot took Miguel

Garcia through the right eye.

The killer was taken to Oxford and tried for murder by a jury that was solely made up of Anglos. They deliberated for twenty minutes and acquitted him. That's what Independence Day meant to Pilar.

Taylor washed some of the desert out of his skin and sat down to eat. Pilar wasn't talking; maybe thinking about Miguel. She was a few years older than Taylor, a handsome woman rather than a beautiful one. There might be some Indian in her; there was a Navaho look about her, in the blue-blackness of her hair; in her high, arrogant cheek-bones, but that didn't worry Taylor. When he was a youth, he'd lived with an Apache girl. Some people called him a 'squaw man' because of that, though not often to his face. But Pilar was tall and slim so maybe there was more than Indian blood in her; maybe the blood of the Queen of Spain or somebody. Whatever, she had still kept her looks and figure and she was all Taylor wanted in female companionship.

Paco came into the house. He was Pilar's son, fifteen years old. He had Pilar's darkness, but was different otherwise; they said he was the image of his father. If so, Miguel Garcia must have been a good-looking man.

Things had been this way and that between Paco and Taylor, the Anglo stranger moving into Paco's house, taking his father's place in his mother's favours, but lately the boy's resentment seemed to have been easing. But now he glared at Taylor with the same hostility he'd shown the very first day they'd met. And more: hatred maybe. Fear too.

He stared at Taylor but spoke to his mother. 'He's killed Quirino Chavez!'

Pilar gave a little gasp. 'Is that true?'

Taylor pushed his plate away from him. 'Quirino and Vincente were trying to kill me. They jumped me in Dog Canyon.'

'Quirino Chavez!'

Paco's mouth twisted with hatred. 'And now you and the other *gringos* are going to kill Vincente too!'

'I ain't one of the other *gringos*, Paco.'

Paco glared some more. His lips trembled like he was on the verge of tears. '*Gringo!*'

Taylor stood. 'Paco — '

He hadn't meant any harm, but Paco stepped back as if the other was about to lunge at him. Then he turned and ran from the room. Pilar called after him, 'Paco!'

Taylor walked after the boy. He came to the flung open door of the adobe and gazed down the dark street, patched with moonlight. He couldn't see Paco. People seemed to be gathering in little knots on the street. They stared at him. That was unusual enough in itself, folk here were ordinarily polite, not given to staring. He sensed the hostility in their stares.

Taylor decided there wasn't anything wrong with him a few drinks wouldn't fix. Ordinarily he would take his troubles over to the main *cantina* in the village and wash them out there, buying drinks for anyone who'd drink with him, and most would. But not tonight . . . perhaps never again.

Taylor went back into the living-room. Pilar stared at him. 'I told you what would happen, you put on that damn badge!'

'The law — '

'*Gringo* law!'

There was that word again: now Pilar was using it! He reached towards her, to take her arm gently. 'Pilar — '

She flinched away.

Anger warmed in him. 'So you think like Paco now! You think I'm a *gringo* too?'

'Why'd you put on that badge? Why, Taylor? The money?'

He inspected his fingertips. 'Maybe I just like killing folks. I have to do it every so often, otherwise I start to itch.'

'Killing Mexicans!'

'Sure, why not? I'll kill anybody,

'long as they pay me. I'll gun down the local school ma'am, the whole Catholic Church, any stray orphans I see about . . . I ain't picky.' He took her arm. 'You knew what kind of man I was. You knew, and you still let me into your bed!'

She shook her arm free. He glared at her; she wouldn't look at him. He said, 'I'm going into Oxford.'

Pilar still didn't look at him. After a minute he moved to the door. She said, 'Don't forget to say hello to Señora Chavez on your way out of town. Tell her about the *gringo* law. Tell her why you killed her son.'

Taylor glared. He spent another minute trying to think of an answer to that, but couldn't. He left the adobe, crossed to the stables and rode out of Agua Frio.

★ ★ ★

As Taylor left Agua Frio, the Regulators came to the Posada de Gallo, the

Inn of the Cock. This inn was the principal building in a one-street adobe settlement too meagre to merit a name — what they call an *ejido* in New Mexico. The Regulators entered the inn noisily, the Arizona Kid leading, and sat at the long tables. The outlaws were all young men, heavily armed, dressed Anglo and Mexican or a mixture of both. They had cruelly humorous, reckless faces, teeth very white against flesh dark from sun and weather.

At the Kid's left hand sat his main lieutenant, Jesse Rudabaugh, at thirty-two the oldest of the Regulators. At his right was the youngest, Red Tom Flynn, only seventeen. Facing the Kid were Tenderfoot Bob McSween and Pecos Joe Evans.

An elderly Mexican couple ran the inn. The Regulators ordered food and told their hosts to, 'Chalk it up!'

The old woman glared at them. She said, 'You no pay.'

Nino grinned. 'Sure we don't pay,

36

honey. We're gentlemen of the road, we don't pay!'

The woman spat.

Jesse Rudabaugh told the innkeeper, 'You ought to learn her some manners, *hombre*.'

'Sure. I know it.'

Nino laughed and declared, 'What, Jesse? Don't you admire a woman with spirit? I surely do.'

Rudabaugh inspected the toe of his boot. He'd got his nose slightly broken somewhere, and wore several days' trail-dust and trail beard; for all that, he was a very handsome man, dark complexioned, with black curling hair. He said, 'It's like Calvin Taylor. I can't figure him. He has a woman like Pilar Garcia at home, you'd think he'd be happy to stay there, not out here, chasing us, dodging lead.'

'Taylor's like us. He's a *bravo* — wild. A quiet life at home ain't for him. He likes guns too much, and what they do.' The Kid took his own gun from its holster and turned it in his hands. It was a double action Colt .41, the model called the Thunderer. He made a small sound of pain and rubbed his right thigh. 'Maybe there's rain coming.'

'You figger?'

'This old wound of mine's acting up. Only time I ever got shot. You remember?'

Jesse nodded. 'Old Buckshot Krauss, wasn't it?'

'That's right. Buckshot Krauss. I owe that Dutchy one.'

The innkeeper brought more food. The woman came with drinks, still glaring at the Regulators. As she moved away, Rudabaugh ran his quirt through his hands. He said, 'What shall we do now? Go into Oxford and shoot it up a little?'

Tom Flynn tugged a strand of his red hair. 'We could go over to the fort and shoot a few of them soldiers.'

Bob McSween chewed his thumbnail. 'Or we could go over to the reservation and steal some horses.'

Pecos Joe Evans stroked his beard. 'Plenty cattle to rustle. We could rob the stage.'

The Kid rubbed his thigh. 'I know what we can do.'

'What?'

'Go and settle up with Buckshot Krauss. He's out at Axtell's sawmill, last I heard.'

The Regulators seemed to think that was a pretty good idea. They got up from the tables. The Kid told the proprietor, 'See you.' The man said, '*Adios*.' His woman scowled. The Kid smiled at her and pinched her cheek, but she flinched away. She said, 'You no pay.'

The Kid laughed and led the others outside. The Regulators rode south out of the settlement. A few miles along, they came across a lone horseman waiting for them: a very young man.

Bob McSween asked this newcomer, 'What you want, kid?'

Jesse Rudabaugh said, 'I'll tell you what he wants: to come along with us. I already told him a few times he'd best run home to his mama. Come back when he's got a few more years.'

The Arizona Kid said, 'It's all right, Jesse. He can come along with us, if he wants.'

'But he ain't hardly frying size!'

'I was younger than him when I got started.'

Tom Flynn grinned. 'Sure I heard that story. You was only twelve when you killed your first man! For insulting your mother. Or was it eleven?'

The Kid grinned back. 'Eleven nothing! I was a baby, hardly one year old when I killed my first man. Shot the son of a bitch for rocking my cradle too violent!'

All the Regulators thought that was hilarious, including the Kid. When he got his laughter under control, the newcomer asked him, 'So I can come along with you?'

The Kid slapped him on the back. 'Sure! If you're crazy enough!'

The boy found a grin of his own. 'Thanks Kid.'

'But where's your mama's boyfriend? Why'n't you bring Calvin Taylor along?'

Paco Garcia scowled. 'That son of a bitch!'

That brought more laughter. The Regulators wheeled their horses and dashed off, Paco following.

4

Taylor rode to Oxford, twenty miles north and east of Agua Frio, arriving at dusk. Like most towns in the South-west, this had once been a sleepy Mexican settlement of adobes and *jacals*, named after a Spanish saint, but the Anglo presence had inexorably, if slowly, asserted itself. The original name had been replaced and forgotten; there were more houses of brick and timber, more businesses advertising in English, not Spanish; more Anglos on the street.

The county town stood in a gap of the mountains, its pretty location and its quaint English name belying its recent bloody history. But now the Oxford County Cattle War was over, even if peace was yet to come.

Taylor spoke to his deputies, the mayor and the undertaker in that order. Then he went to the two-storey adobe that passed for the sheriff's office and jailhouse. He questioned the only prisoner — Vincente Chavez — and got little satisfaction. Then he sat down and ate the meal that was brought over. His thoughts got in the way of his appetite and he left the food half-finished. He poured himself two fingers of fairly bad whiskey and sat in his swivel chair, his bootheels resting on the upended crate that served as a desk, nursing the whiskey and brooding on things, Pilar most of all. When there was a knock on the door, Taylor's hand jumped to the gun on his hip; he gave a noise of self-disgust. He unbuckled the gunbelt and laid it on the desk before him, the cedar grip of the pistol still within reach. He said, 'Come in.'

A stranger came into the room. A man about thirty-five, middle-sized, stocky, city-dressed in broadcloth suit and derby. He had a square, cleft-chinned face, freckled like a boy, and skin too fair to have been out in this sun long. The eyes behind the spectacles were blue, bright with intelligence.

'Sheriff Taylor? You don't know me —'

'Right both times.'

'I'm new in town. In the territory, for that matter.'

'From the East?'

The other nodded. 'Emmet J. Rhodes.' He extended his hand and they shook. For all Rhodes' soft looks, the grip was surprisingly firm. 'I just started with *The Oxford County Chronicle*.'

Taylor sighed. 'Newspaperman?'

'That's right, sir. I wondered if you could spare me the time for a brief interview.'

'My time's mighty pressing,' Taylor lied. 'But if you can be brief —'

'Assuredly.'

Taylor indicated a chair, the journalist sat. He removed his derby, revealing a crop of springy, rust-coloured hair. He produced notebook and pencil. 'You certainly seem to have made an impression already in your new job.

Already gunsmoke in Dog Canyon — '

'You was keeping it brief Mr Rhodes . . . '

'Assuredly.' The newspaperman opened his notebook. 'Now, before we come to the Arizona Kid, I'd like a few biographical details . . . '

'Uh?'

'Your own illustrious past . . . up to and including your spectacular deeds in Dog Canyon.'

Taylor studied the cigarette he'd shaped. 'Spectacular?'

'Your full name is . . . '

'Taylor, Calvin Taylor.' The sheriff made an impatient sound. 'I thought you wanted to know about the Kid?'

Taylor was hinting as broadly as he could that his own past was a closed book; a hint Rhodes seemed to take, as his next remark was, 'Then perhaps we can begin with filling in a little background. The Oxford County Cattle War — '

Taylor sighed once more. 'Too complicated to explain. To cut it simple: two lots of cattlemen fighting about money. Each side got up a private army, some real cowboys and some hired guns. The Kid was part of a gang called themselves the Regulators.'

'Wasn't he their leader?'

Taylor shook his head. 'No, he was third or fourth down the ladder. Only the fellers above him tended to get themselves killed; so, eventually, after the Regulators was whittled down some, Nino found himself leader. By which time the war was over and the Kid's side had lost. But what was left of the Regulators carried on stealing horses and cattle like the war was still on. Which is where I come in.'

'Ah yes, the Kid . . . or is it Nino? El Chivato? You know him well?'

'Drank with him, played cards with him, seen him around cockfights, *bailes* and such.'

'What do you feel about him?'

'Personally? I like him.'

Rhodes gave him a surprised look.

'Really. This man they call The Terror in His Teens?'

Taylor smiled. 'Who knows why you like some people? You just do.'

Rhodes licked the stub of his pencil. 'The Kid was born, I believe, in the Irish slums of New York.'

'Indiana, he once told me. or was it Missouri?'

'Real name Billy — '

'Henry McCarthy.'

Rhodes swallowed. 'The Kid came into the territory from Arizona.'

'You got that part right.'

A man blundered into the office. Taylor had already dragged the Colt from the belt on his desk, had it centred on the midsection of the newcomer — which was a fair-sized target.

Taylor said, 'Curly, my nerves been all to hell lately, so you'd better learn to knock before you bust in!'

Curly — the nickname was a perverse joke, given his baldness — nodded his shining, domelike pate. 'Sorry Sheriff.'

Taylor smiled grimly. *Sheriff*. He

was still getting used to the title.

'But it's the Kid!'

'Nino?'

The deputy nodded again. 'A rider just got in. Murder's being done over at Axtell's Mill! The Kid and his gang — they're killing old Buckshot Krauss!'

5

Werner Krauss had been in the wars. In fact he'd been in so many wars he couldn't remember them all. In every one, he'd presented a big target: he stood a head above six feet, a hulking man with arms like cabers. He had a great red face and fierce grey beard that spilled on to his barrel chest. A quarter-century of soldiering — for the British in India, for or against Garibaldi in Italy (he couldn't remember which), for Maximilian in Mexico — had left its mark: a dragging limp from a lance thrust in the left leg; his nose broken and flattened to his face by a sabre cut; his forehead permanently furrowed by a bullet scar. Even supposedly peaceful pursuits had scarred him: a stint of buffalo hunting on the High Plains had left the barbed iron tip of a Kiowa arrow in his right shoulder. Most recently, during another unofficial war — the one in Oxford County — he'd picked up a load of buckshot in his other shoulder that made his left-hand fingers slow, and won him his nickname.

Now Buckshot was riding up to an imposing two-storey adobe building. Axtell's sawmill. In between wars, Krauss earned a dollar clerking for Axtell, although, thinking of the work ahead of him, sorting out Axtell's business accounts, he decided he'd rather face grapeshot or a cavalry charge than a ledger full of numbers.

Krauss reined in his mule and dismounted. And paused. He didn't know why he didn't just walk over to the office, but some instinct held him there, at the hitching rail. He studied the adobe before him, the empty corrals nearby, the surrounding country. He saw nothing amiss. And yet . . . Buckshot cradled his battered Winchester, touched the grip of his Colt pistol and strode towards the sawmill.

50

A man came around the corner of the building towards him. Krauss halted, seeing an old enemy from the recent Oxford County hostilities — Jesse Rudabaugh. Jesse said, 'We've come to settle up, Buckshot.'

Krauss noted the *we*. His voice still heavy with its German accent, he said, 'Do your worst. Where's the Kid? I'll settle with that little son of a bitch.'

'He ain't here.'

Buckshot sneered, 'You are a god-damned liar, Jesse — '

Jesse grabbed for the pistol in his scabbard. Krauss swung the Winchester and fired. He caught the man dead centre and Jesse was knocked backwards, went sprawling. To Krauss's astonishment, Jesse sat up almost instantly, his pistol in his hand. He fired. Krauss felt the bullet punch into his midsection. Strength was chopped from his legs and he fell headlong. He ploughed into the dust on his chin. There was sand and blood in his mouth. He was hit badly, but he felt no pain, only numbness, shock, astonishment. Suddenly, he felt a surge of anger, too, lying there like a poleaxed steer with maybe his death on him. After all he'd been through, to be finished by a cheap desperado like Rudabaugh! Out of his chest came a feral bellow of rage.

Rudabaugh staggered to his feet, his hands pressed to his side. Krauss saw his belt was askew, the Winchester bullet had glanced from his belt buckle: the Devil's luck! From somewhere, Buckshot found the strength to push himself from the earth; he struggled to his knees. Men had appeared from behind the building, were running towards him: more of the Regulators. He saw the Arizona Kid amongst them and his lips worked back in a savage grin. Buckshot used the Winchester to lever himself to his feet; then he raised the weapon and began to fire as fast as he was able. The Regulators shot at him; a bullet raked his left side. But his rapid fire broke their charge, they veered towards cover. He chopped down a running man. This man pitched headlong, falling through a corral fence pole, kept rolling.

Buckshot yelled, 'Come on, you sons of bitches!'

The Regulators didn't oblige. Krauss turned and moved towards the office, although he seemed to be dragging his boots through knee-high mud. Feet slapped the earth behind him; he turned. Two Regulators were running at him flat out; the Kid was the nearest.

Buckshot jerked his Winchester to the hip. He squeezed trigger and the hammer punched an empty! The Kid's face broke into a wild, triumphant grin; he raised his pistol and worked the trigger. A misfire! By now he was at full sprint, coming at Krauss head on. He began to veer aside and Krauss lunged with his rifle, driving the barrel into the Kid's belly. Nino gasped, doubled forward and plunged headlong. The Regulator behind him leapt in, a knife showing in his hand. Krauss flung his Winchester, which caught his attacker across the face and brought him down, skidding on his back. He writhed off the earth and Buckshot kicked him in the throat. By now the old German had freed his pistol from its scabbard and fired at the other Regulators, who went hunting cover. This gave Krauss a minute to back into the office and slam the door.

Once that was done, Buckshot fell face down on the floor. He was surprised to discover he was lying in a lake of his own blood, that his shirt and pants were sodden with it. It wouldn't be long then, before he fainted from loss of blood, and then they'd finish him . . . if he lived that long.

At first Buckshot couldn't move his body or legs, all he could move was his head which he turned slowly, ranging his gaze over the bare room. To his surprise, he saw a rifle leaning against the wall. A single-shot Sharps, calibre 50.170, a fabled 'Big Fifty': old Axtell's buffalo-killing gun. Now if he could only reach it . . .

★ ★ ★

The Regulators huddled together in an irrigation ditch in front of the adobe, just at the edge of rifle range. Now and then one of them would raise up and take a quick peek at the building. Jesse Rudabaugh rubbed his side, bruised and ripped from the bullet that had flattened and torn away his belt buckle and skated over his left-side ribs. Red Tom Flynn rubbed his throat where Krauss's boot had caught him. Black-eye bruising had already started across his cheeks where he'd been caught by the old man's rifle. The Kid rubbed the aching in the pit of his stomach, where the rifle barrel had gone into him like a sword. He asked, 'How you doing, Bob?'

Bob McSween coughed, and blood came from his mouth. He pressed a hand to his right-side ribs where the bullet had caught him. 'I figger he's killed me.'

'Hell,' the Kid said. 'That's too bad.'

Pecos Joe Evans stood. He said, 'I wonder what old Buckshot's doing now?'

Flynn said, 'I wouldn't rise up like that, Joe.'

'He's only got a pistol, he can't hit me at this range.' Joe climbed from the ditch.

Rudabaugh snorted. 'That old bastard — he can't hold out long. I killed him sure.'

Flynn said, 'But while we're waiting for him to die, Taylor could be coming down on us with a posse. You sure you trust that Paco, Kid?'

Nino chewed a stalk of grama grass smiling. 'Sure. Paco's a good boy.' He addressed Evans, who was striding towards the adobe. 'Don't get too close, Joe.'

Evans halted. He turned towards his companions. 'Like I said, he's only got a pistol.' He grinned and his face exploded. He began to fall.

The Regulators flung themselves flat. The gunshot was deafening. Tom Flynn put his hands to his ears. He asked, 'Christ, what was that? Sounded like a cannon!'

His face to the earth, Rudabaugh said, 'I'll tell you what that was — that was a Sharps. Krauss's got hold of a buffalo gun!'

The idea of facing so terrible a weapon made even men as hard as these gasp; despite that, the Kid risked lifting from the earth long enough to snatch a quick glance at the adobe.

Flynn asked, 'How's Joe?'

The Kid took a moment replying. 'I figure Krauss must have hit poor old Joe in the head. Leastways, that's the only part of him that's missing.'

Rudabaugh said, 'Jesus Christ! Let's vamoose!'

The Regulators got ready to move. McSween said, 'You'd better leave me, boys. I ain't got long.'

The Kid glanced over at Jesse, who had begun to lift his pistol from its scabbard. He shook his head slightly and Jesse let the gun slide back into place.

McSween tried to smile. 'The next face I see'll be Joe's.'

The Kid grinned. 'Unlikely. He ain't got one. You should see Krauss though. Maybe you'll last long enough to say hello to Mr Taylor if he shows up.'

Jesse said, 'Put a bullet in the son of a bitch for me. We had us some times, Bob.'

'*Adios*, boys.'

Leaving McSween sitting in his blood, the other Regulators moved from the ditch and reached cover without the buffalo gun seeking them out. They entered a dry wash.

Jesse told the Kid, 'Maybe I should've let Bob out of his pain.'

Nino rubbed his bruised stomach. 'Why waste cartridges?'

At the end of the wash Paco waited, standing watch over the Regulators' horses. He grinned at the returning men. 'You get that Buckshot?'

Jesse scowled. 'I figure we finished him.'

Paco's grin slipped. 'Where's Joe and Bob?'

Nino swung himself up into the saddle of his bay mare. He said. 'They ain't coming.'

6

Calvin Taylor's posse formed on the streets of Oxford. Taylor studied his deputies gloomily. Eyeing the three Yerby brothers, his lips tightened in disgust. Curly was all right, but slow-witted and fat, out of condition. Pat O'Keefe was the only man here he'd've chosen to ride with, if he had his druthers. But beggars couldn't be choosers . . .

A voice said, 'I'm volunteering.' Taylor was surprised to see the news-paperman, Emmet Rhodes, riding up. Rhodes had changed from his city gear to canvas jacket and pants, his derby replaced by a pith helmet. He was riding a grey horse Taylor liked the look of, and there was a Winchester in his saddle scabbard.

Taylor said, 'I didn't invite you along.'

'I invited myself.'

The sheriff said, 'We might have a long trail ahead of us into some bad country. The Regulators got a hide-out in the White Sands.'

The possemen frowned, thinking about entering this dread place. Taylor went on, 'And most of those we're up against have killed their man — all save the younker, Flynn.'

Zeke said, 'We don't need no tenderfoot with us we got to nurse-maid.'

Rhodes smiled a little. 'Perhaps you misjudge me, sir. I can ride and shoot. I served in the war with the Second Battalion, Eighteenth Infantry. I fought at Stone's River.'

O'Keefe gave Rhodes a sharp look. 'That was a good outfit I hear.'

Taylor said, 'You might be after a story, Rhodes, but we're after armed killers. If you can't keep up, ain't nobody going to help you.'

Rhodes nodded. 'Fair enough.'

'You must've been pretty young,

fighting in the war.'

'I lied about my age.'

O'Keefe said, 'Well, learning to lie's good training for a newspaperman!' He grinned to show no offence was intended and Rhodes smiled also.

Taylor said, 'We're burning daylight.' He walked over to his horse; the posse rode south out of town.

They came to the Inn of the Cock and were told that the gang had stopped there to eat. Taylor told the proprietor, 'You must've heard 'em talking. They say just where they were going next?'

The innkeeper wouldn't meet Taylor's eye. 'I don't hear what they say.'

As the posse moved outside, Taylor told Rhodes, 'The Kid's got everybody scared.'

Rhodes shook his head. 'Robbing coaches. Taking over and terrorizing settlements. They don't bother to wear gunnysacks over their heads, or masks, or anything. Just carry on in broad daylight like a bunch of high-spirited youths, not afraid of anything. Isn't there any law in this country?'

Taylor smiled. 'Sure. We're it.'

The posse rode south once more. Even though they were supposed to be dashing to the rescue of Buckshot Krauss, Taylor held down the pace; it was too easy to wear out horses over this kind of country, in this heat. A mile or so along, more sign showed up on the trail. Zeke and Taylor dismounted to inspect it.

Zeke said, 'Looks like another rider joined 'em. Should be easy to track this one's horse. Near front hoof split. Anybody know those tracks? Sheriff?'

Taylor didn't reply and Zeke grinned. He fancied himself a better outdoorsman/tracker than Taylor. Taylor judged Zeke to be the brains of the family, though just as mean as his brothers, and was therefore the most dangerous. He certainly knew how to run a trail. It was rumoured he'd been a scalp-hunter down in Mexico back when bounty was still paid on Indian hair. A dirty trade; it was calculated that for every five scalps delivered, only one was the genuine article, the scalp of an Apache fighting man. The other four were the scalps of women or children, or peaceful Indians, or even Mexicans.

Zeke declared, 'Riding light, whoever it is. Only boy-size maybe. What you figure, Taylor?'

Taylor frowned; he said nothing.

The posse approached Axtell's sawmill; buzzards marked the place, turning slow spirals in the sky. The horsemen entered a bosky, or grove of mesquite trees on a hump of ground overlooking the mill and reined in. Taylor scanned the land before them with his field glasses. 'I can see one down. By the corrals there.'

Mose said, 'Let's go see!' He kicked his horse into movement, Sam began to follow.

Taylor told them, 'I don't figure how you boys've lived so long.'

The two Yerbys reined in their horses. They glared at the lawman.

Taylor smiled. 'Somebody's still alive

down there, otherwise those buzzards'd be down on the ground, having lunch.'

Zeke smiled too. 'That's right, boys.'

The possemen shifted uneasily in their saddles, checking their guns, expecting Regulator fire any second.

Rhodes pointed. 'I thought I saw metal flash. Over there in that irrigation ditch.'

Taylor raised the field glasses to his face once more. 'You got sharp eyes, Rhodes. Man with a rifle sitting in that ditch.' He gazed at Mose. 'Just waiting for you and Sam.'

O'Keefe asked, 'Can you see Buckshot?'

Taylor shook his head. He handed the field glasses to the Irishman and dismounted. 'Pat, you keep prospecting this country with those glasses. The rest of you wait here. I'm going to kind of sneak up on our friend there, with a view to taking him alive if possible.' He discarded his boots. Taking a pair of Apache moccasins — deerskin boots that reached above the knee — from his saddle-bags, he pulled them on.

Sam asked, 'What if the Regulators *are* still about. What if they jump you?'

'Then I expect you all to hasten to my aid with all despatch.'

The possemen, even the Yerbys, smiled at that. Rhodes said, 'I'll come with you. We can take him on both sides.'

Taylor said, 'You can't turn in your story if you get killed.'

Sam declared, 'Hell, let him go. After all, he lied about his age just so he could get to be a war hero.'

Taylor and Rhodes moved forward, their rifles in their hands. They kept to cover and came to the main building. Taylor took a glance through the one glassless window. Buckshot Krauss lay on his back in the centre of the room, sprawled in a great puddle of his own blood. If he was still breathing, Taylor couldn't hear it. Glimpsing Rhodes moving forward through a belt of saltbrush, Taylor indicated: keep moving forward, I will too.

He came up on the irrigation ditch from the left; Rhodes approached from the right. There was a shot; Rhodes tumbled forward, somersaulting into the ditch. Taylor sprang into the ditch, landing with his legs braced and dived headlong, ploughing into the earth on his elbows. He jammed his rifle into his shoulder. He saw, through brush, the dim bulk of a man with his back to him, squinting along a rifle. Taylor got to his feet and ran forward; the rifleman turned towards him. Taylor ducked into cover behind a log, fixing his enemy in his sights. The man was moving with the agonizing slowness of a crippled thing. Taylor could have shot him a dozen times before he came even half about. Instead, the sheriff stood and walked over to him. Taylor recognized Tenderfoot Bob McSween.

As Taylor approached, McSween grinned. There was blood on his teeth. He tried to lift his rifle, to aim the Winchester at the lawman's midsection, but couldn't manage it. The sheriff leaned forward and took the rifle from McSween's hands.

Taylor heard approaching feet. Emmet Rhodes appeared, his rifle in his hands. Taylor said, 'I figured you was killed.'

'Not quite.' Rhodes lifted his hand to his right ear and felt at it gingerly; his fingertips came away with blood on them.

The sheriff climbed from the ditch. He waved his hat, a signal for the rest of the posse to join them. He got interested in tracks which led him to a wash to the south. There horses had stood, undoubtedly the Regulators' animals. He walked back to the posse who were standing around Bob McSween. He asked them, 'How's Krauss?'

Zeke told him, 'Dead.'

McSween groaned. Taylor asked him, 'That Pecos Joe dead in the corral there?'

After a moment of trying, McSween

68

found the strength to speak. 'Sure. Can't you see?'

'He's kind of hard to recognize. Can you drink some water?'

'I don't want nothing from any of you bastards.'

Mose kicked the man's leg. O'Keefe turned towards Yerby, outrage in his face. He said, 'Why, you son of a bitch!'

Mose sneered, 'You on me again, long-legs? You don't want this scum to suffer — fine.' Mose produced his pistol, cocked it, aimed it at the wounded man's face. 'Take your medicine, Bob.'

McSween called, 'Oh Jesus Christ!'

Taylor stared at the back of his hands. 'Put the gun away, Mose.'

'I'm only doing him a mercy.'

'Put the gun away.'

Mose studied the lawman's face and thought about it. Nobody moved or spoke for at least a minute. Then Mose shrugged and pushed his Colt back in its holster. He walked over to his horse.

Taylor squatted by the dying man, positioning himself so his shadow kept McSween's face out of the sun. 'Hey, Bob, you won five dollars off me once, in a monte game in Agua Frio. You remember? I figured you was cheating.'

'That's right; I was,' McSween grinned. 'I'll pay you back next week.' Taylor grinned too.

O'Keefe told McSween: 'Face it, Bob. You're killed. You might as well tell us where the Kid has run to. Where he hides out. Get it off your conscience.'

'Go to hell.'

The Irishman frowned. 'Now Bob, you don't want to die with a curse on your lips.'

But that's what McSween did; he swore at O'Keefe and died while he was doing it.

Taylor said, 'Gone to hell with five dollars and ten cents of my good money.' He leaned forward and closed the dead man's eyes.

Zeke said, 'That old Dutchy sure made his fight! He whipped those sons of bitches!'

Taylor made a sound of agreement. 'Rest of 'em'll be twice as mean, now they've got wounds to lick. We'll go back to the inn and outfit, then get after 'em. Those of you want to come along. It might be a hard business from now on, chasing 'em.'

O'Keefe asked, 'You reckon?'

Taylor nodded. 'It's like I thought. Tracks point south-west. Into the *malpais*. They're heading into the White Sands.'

7

The Regulators had crossed the bleached wastes of the White Sands. They were half-blind from the dazzling of the salt-white earth; they had gritty dust in their eyes, mouths, hair, between their fingers, everywhere, the harsh, metallic taste of gypsum in their mouths. They were dazed from the heat, their clothing rank with sweat. But the hell of the White Sands was their protection — no posse had ever dared pursue them across it. At the end of their journey they came to their safe haven.

The Regulators' hide-out was an abandoned swing station for a failed stage line. The house stood where the brilliant waves of the White Sands washed up against the front range of the San Andres Mountains. A substantial two-room adobe with a roof of mesquite thatch, the corral behind the house had adobe walls built tall and strong against thieves.

The outlaws had shot a sheep *en route* and someone got busy cooking it. They had all the cowman's prejudices against sheepmen and their flocks. Normally they wouldn't touch mutton, but today they were hungry. There was a spring nearby that sometimes issued foul, alkalied water, and got the place its name, Dirty Springs or Bad Water. A man couldn't drink this water, unless there was no alternative, and today there was none.

The other two Regulators were there: Dutch Swebke and Jose Maria Baca.

The Arizona Kid stood off by himself. He took a rag and began to clean the dust out of his pistol and rifle. Occasionally he'd pause and gaze off into the distance.

Jesse Rudabaugh watched the Kid. He shaped a cigarette and passed the makings to Paco Garcia and Tom Flynn. He said, 'That's the Kid for you. Some of us think of our bellies first, or our horses, or get some sleep. Me, I'd like a bath. But Nino — first thing he does is look to his guns. There's another little trick he does. You know those fancy fringed gloves he wears sometimes? If he starts playing with 'em, or puts 'em on, that means he's in the mood for killing. Ready to go to his guns. Doesn't always do it, that'd tip the other fellow off, but . . . you see him playing with those gloves, watch out.'

Paco asked, 'You known the Kid a long time?'

Jesse smiled. 'Nobody knows the Kid. Something you ought to think about. In case you get to thinking you and him are friends. The Kid always looks after himself first. He never lets anyone get close to him. Too dangerous.' Jesse rasped his nails through the salt dust in his trail beard. 'He's changed though.'

'How do you mean?'

'Something's happened to him. Like with McSween. I wanted to put Bob out of his pain but all the Kid said was, 'Why waste cartridges'? He'd rather leave Bob there with a bullet in the guts. He wasn't like that once. He's changing. I think maybe he's scared.'

'The Kid? You're crazy!'

'He thinks Taylor's the one man might finish him. That's why he's getting meaner and harder. Hell,' Jesse grinned. 'He might even end up something like me.' The wind lifted, sifting white soil towards them. Jesse frowned. 'I just hope there ain't a blower coming.'

* * *

The Oxford posse night-camped on the north-eastern rim of the White Sands. There had been a high wind all day; the posse had taken shelter from it in a little high-walled canyon. They ate their evening meal listening to the bleary howling of the gale, crashing like the sea against the world outside the canyon.

75

Zeke Yerby picked a sliver of meat from between his teeth. 'We can't go out on the sands while this blower keeps up. Them Regulators'll get clean away.'

Sam fed another mesquite root into the campfire. 'I don't figure they're out there anyway. I reckon the Kid's doubled back on us. He'll be in Agua Frio right now, lying in a nice, comfortable bed, laughing at us damn fools.'

Taylor poured coffee for himself. The first cold of the night sneaked along the flesh of his arm and he pulled his canvas jacket tighter about him. 'Why Agua Frio?'

'He's got a Mex gal there.'

'Which one? He's got more sweethearts on the creek than a little.'

'I'd heard Celsa Chavez is the latest.'

Taylor frowned. If the Kid was squiring the Chavez girl it might explain Vincente and Quirino's part in this, as Celsa was their sister.

Emmet Rhodes came and sat

76

alongside him. He said, 'Sheriff — '

'You want the rest of your interview? Well . . . all right.'

'It seemed to annoy you — the last time we talked.'

Taylor listened to the dull booming of the wind beyond the canyon. 'It's just that you get all these made-up stories. In the yellow-back novels. Damn trash. It makes jokes out of all of us.'

Rhodes produced notebook and pencil. 'We were discussing the Kid. Barely twenty years old yet has killed a man for every year of his life.'

'I figure the Kid's twenty-four, twenty-five. He was in on five or six gang killings.'

'What about the Kid shooting down Sheriff Kelly in a face-to-face contest?'

Taylor rolled a cigarette. 'A bunch of Regulators was hiding behind a wall when Kelly rode past, they fair peppered him. Cut him down from behind.'

'But didn't the Kid personally despatch the two killers of that English rancher?

What was his name? Challenged both to a duel, then shot them dead one after the other.'

'Another gang killing. Both of those was shot when they was prisoners; fair ventilated by eight or nine guns. Probably the Kid was one of 'em did it.'

Rhodes snapped his notebook closed. 'Well, thank you, Sheriff. You've done a fair job of debunking.'

'De — what?'

'Cutting the legend down to size. El Chivato seems to be a fairly minor, squalid stock thief and assassin; in the killing stakes pretty small beer alongside the likes of, say . . . Clay Allison or Bill Longley or John Wesley Hardin.'

Taylor considered the men Rhodes had named. 'Mean sons of bitches.'

'So why the big legend about a relatively minor figure like the Kid?'

'You tell me.'

Rhodes thought a moment. 'Maybe it's the idea of the doomed youth who has to pay for his glorious life with his early, violent death . . . sort of a sun god who has to burn out young . . . like Cuchullain.'

Taylor coughed over his cigarette. 'Cu — what? Mister, there's a bottle of fairly bad whiskey over there — you better clear that word out of your throat! I'd hate for it to get stuck there!'

Lifting his voice against the rising wind, Mose said, 'There's one good thing about that blower. Hey, Curly?'

Curly looked up from his plate. His mouth full of food, he said, 'Huh?'

'That blower, it means there ain't likely to be any wild Indians about.'

'Wild Indians?'

'Sure. Don't believe everything you hear about the Mescaleros being pacified. They're out there right now, sharpening up their scalping knives ready for the next white-eye they catch.'

Curly grinned and touched his bald head. 'They gonna be out of luck they try and scalp me!'

79

Taylor said, 'Mose is just joking you, Curly. The Mescaleros is all peaceful now.'

Sam smirked. 'Well, you should know. You're the real Apache expert.'

Mose said, 'Expert on their *women*,' and laughed. He spoke out of the side of his mouth to his brothers, but every man around the campfire heard him.

Taylor felt a quick pulse of anger. He saw O'Keefe and the others watching him, waiting for him to act. But he couldn't: he was the sheriff; the star pinned to the left side of his shirt said so. It was his job to hold this posse together. He touched the dull tin of the badge, felt the gritty sand in his hair and flesh, the acrid taste of gypsum in his mouth; he remembered the Yerbys sitting and laughing and looking over at him; he thought about Paco and Pilar . . . the anger became bigger and warmer inside him. He stood slowly. 'You mean something by that, Mose?'

Mose stood, too. He studied the sheriff as if deciding how to play this;

then, having judged the other man, he smiled. 'Why, nothing. No offence intended.'

'All right.'

Yerby's smile widened. 'Just that everyone knows you ain't picky about the sort of women you go with. You don't care if they're Mex, red — '

He turned to grin at his brothers and Taylor flung what was left of his coffee in Mose's face. It was cold, but Mose didn't know that, he yelled like he was being scalded. While he was yelling, Taylor hit him. It was a looping right cross that took Mose along the jaw and spun him backwards. He went down.

Men by the fire scrambled clear as Mose rolled in dust, then struggled up. Taylor sprang at him; swept off his hat and slashed Mose across the face with it, four or five times. His eyes screwed tight, Mose cried out. Taylor dropped his hat, bunched his fists and launched a right jab that rocked Mose back on his heels. Taylor swung again. This time his aim was off, he caught

Mose in the throat. Mose choked and clutched his neck, sinking to his knees, swaying there; for a second it looked like he'd topple forward into the fire.

Taylor stepped towards his enemy, suddenly aware that Sam was behind him. He turned and saw Sam crouched, ready to strike. His teeth were bared and the firelight played on the knife in his hand.

There was the sound of a gun being cocked. O'Keefe said, 'It's not your fight, Yerby.'

Sam glared at O'Keefe. Zeke said, 'Leave these scrapping fools to fight, Sam.'

Sam glared some more, then he slid his knife back into its sheath. Taylor was watching Sam and not Mose. Mose came off the ground with his hands full of white ashes from the campfire. He flung these at Taylor's face. The sheriff sprang back, dodging some of the ashes, but not all of them. Warm dust went into his eyes, blinding him. He cried out. Mose charged him. His shoulder caught Taylor's chest, bowling the other man from his feet. Taylor fell and Mose's fingers closed around his throat. Still blind, Taylor kicked out; his foot hooked into Yerby's stomach, lifting Mose into the air. Mose somersaulted forward, struck the ground on his head and rolled.

He took a long minute getting to his knees. That gave Taylor time to blink the ashes out of his eyes and rub his throat where Mose's iron fingers had clamped and bitten. Mose glared at him dazedly, his eyes not quite focused, his mouth open and blood on his lips. White dust paled his face. He started to rise. Taylor stood also; he found his legs weren't quite firm under him. Then O'Keefe called, 'There's your wild Indians!'

Taylor turned and looked. Someone stepped from the darkness into the rim of firelight. An Indian: an old man with brindled grey hair that hung to his chest, tied with a rag about his temples.

Curly started to lift his rifle. Taylor said, 'Hold it, Curly!'

Curly asked, 'Is he a Mescalero?' Fear made his voice high.

Zeke Yerby sneered, 'Why, that's Geronimo himself!'

Taylor studied the beautifully patterned blanket the old man had wrapped about himself. 'Looks like a Navaho.' He brushed some ash and dust from his shirt and gazed at Mose. 'You want some more?'

Mose scowled. He rubbed the red mark one of Taylor's punches had left on his jaw and cheek. There was a silence; then he said, 'We can finish this later.'

Taylor nodded, accepting the threat. He spoke to the old man in Spanish, which was the universal language amongst the Indians of the Southwest. Then he told the others, 'He's a Navaho all right. Sheepherder. He's seen some Anglos, wild young men, riding their horses like crazy men. Four of them. Seen them around here before. Figures they're *gringos ladrones*. Most interesting part is he knows where they've gone, where they're hid out. And he'll lead us to 'em, provided we promise to kill them all. He doesn't like white men.'

Zeke studied the Navaho like he was back at his old hair-raising business, like his hand still itched for the scalping knife. 'He doesn't huh?'

'Why should he? The Anglos penned up his people on the Bosque Redondo, promised to feed them, then let them starve. He watched hundreds of 'em die, of cold, hunger, sickness. His wives and children . . . '

'Why should we believe that red bastard? If he hates us like he says, he'll just lead us out into an ambush on the White Sands.'

'No. He hates the *gringos ladrones* more. He's mad at them 'cos they rode through his flock, scattered 'em all over. Shot a few of his sheep for food, some for meanness. He knows a trail leads right to them, goes around the White Sands, not through it.'

O'Keefe rubbed his chin. 'That'd be something. Finding the Kid's roost.'

Taylor nodded. 'According to this old man, we could be on 'em tomorrow night.'

Zeke lifted his coffee cup. 'This expedition might turn out to be some fun after all!'

'I'd like to remind everyone,' Rhodes said, 'that this isn't a hunting party. We're engaged in carrying out the due process of the law. We're here to catch the Kid if possible; we're not paid executioners.'

The Yerbys grinned at each other. Zeke said, 'Sure. The due process of the law.' He rolled a little coffee in his mouth, then he spat carefully into the fire.

8

The wind had blown fitfully all day, now, at dusk, it made low music, sculpting the dunes of the White Sands. The Regulators lay about in the abandoned swing station, talking, smoking or playing cards. The Arizona Kid didn't smoke, instead he chewed a wad of tobacco. He lay on the earth floor of the adobe, his hands cupped behind his head, gazing at the low ceiling.

At his side, Jesse Rudabaugh said, 'Me'n' Tom was talking. Maybe we should quit this country, now the law's breathing so hot on our collars.'

'Quit it for where?'

'Mexico. You know there's no law down there.' Jesse's eyes glimmered with anticipation. 'We could take that whole country.'

The Kid made himself more

comfortable on the floor. 'You want to try Mexico, fine. I like it round here.'

Jesse smiled grudgingly. 'You like Celsa Chavez, you mean.'

'Maybe.'

'She'll get you killed, Kid.'

Nino picked a thread of tobacco from between his teeth. 'If a bullet's got your name on it, that's it. Better than dying of hard work, anyway!'

Jesse said, 'I'll take a look out front.' He moved towards the door.

The Kid practised whistling a favourite tune, 'Silver Threads Amongst The Gold', then he noticed Paco Garcia watching him.

Paco asked, 'You sure it's safe, hanging around here?'

'These horses got to rest. Why did you come with us, Paco?'

'I want to be like you.'

'Why?'

'Seems to me you're the only people in this whole miserable territory who know how to live!'

Nino grinned. 'You might be right

88

at that. But your pa — he was a law-and-order man, I hear. He wouldn't want you to run around with the likes of us.'

'Sure, he was a law-and-order man. Look what it got him.' Paco scowled. 'All the law seems to mean is the Mexican stays poor, the Anglo gets rich. The Mexican knows his place, he gets a plate of beans, maybe, if he forgets it, he gets killed.'

'Get killed our way, too.'

'Nobody gonna kill you, Kid!'

The Kid told Paco, 'Don't put too much store in me, Paco. I'm only the same as anybody else. I might turn out to be a disappointment to you.'

'Sure.'

The Kid laughed. Then there was gunfire.

* * *

At dusk, the Oxford posse were in place, in sight of the Regulators' hideout. Taylor got his men in cover, where they checked their guns. He went ahead and lay just back of a ridge, studying the adobe through his field glasses. There was still plenty of shooting light although shadows were capturing the lower slopes of the mountains and the wind, raising an ashen curtain before the house, played strange games with visibility.

O'Keefe, Rhodes, Curly and Zeke came to join the sheriff. He told them, 'Six horses in the corral, so maybe Dutch Swebke and Jose Baca are down there. We might be up against the whole gang.'

The others frowned, considering this. Taylor went on, 'I'd like to go in before full dark, but maybe there's not time. I don't like the idea of waiting for daylight, too much could spook them before then, but maybe we'll have to.'

Curly said, 'We could burn 'em out. Coal oil 'em!'

Taylor pulled a face. 'Likely get

picked off before you could get close enough.'

Curly scowled like a thwarted child. Taylor said, 'One thing though: the Kid shows outside that 'dobe, we kill him instant.'

Rhodes said, 'You mean if he doesn't surrender we kill him.'

'You want us to call out 'Throw up your hands', something like that?'

'That's right.'

Taylor shook his head. 'We see the Kid, we cut him down. We can holler after. These ain't Reb soldiers we're up against, Rhodes.'

'They're still men, not animals.'

'We get the Kid, the rest of 'em'll quit. Even Jesse Rudabaugh. We don't, they got a strong place to fight from. Six men and they all know how to use guns. That's *all* they know. I didn't bring this posse out here to get them killed.'

'Some people would call what you're planning murder.'

'Put it in your newspaper.'

Rhodes glared. 'I will.'

O'Keefe hissed, 'Something's happening!'

Taylor slewed around. The steerhide door of the adobe started to open. Taylor gestured to the men with him, a wide sweep of his arm saying, *get down*. He sank to the earth and pulled his rifle to his shoulder; around him men did the same. Curly moved to the left, towards the cover of some boulders. Taylor fixed an aim on the doorway, waiting for Curly to get in place before he fired. Then he saw Curly was too high on the ridge, where he could be seen. Taylor felt a surge of anger; he opened his mouth to yell at Curly to keep his fool head down.

Curly tripped. He fell sprawling on the rubbled slope, starting a little rock slide. His rifle flew ahead of him, clattering on loose stones. He cried out.

A dim shape showed in the doorway and Taylor fired. *Fired and knew he'd missed*. In his ears other rifles sounded, one simultaneous roar, cracking open the world, deafening him. Bullets hammered into the adobe wall, the steerhide door, but they were too late, the Regulator was inside, the door slammed to.

Curly scrambled up the slope towards the posse. Rifles cracked from the adobe. Curly yelled and stumbled and fell headlong. He landed on the ridge and spilled down the slope beyond it. The posse returned fire; for a minute the darkening world was brilliant with the lightning flashes of rifles, noisy with the crashing of guns. Then both sides quit shooting.

Taylor turned his head and saw Curly sprawled on the slope behind them. For a moment he thought the man was dead, then the posseman got to his knees. He winced with pain. Taylor asked him, 'You hit?'

Curly touched his right buttock. He lifted bloody fingers. 'Creased me in the — '

Zeke sneered, 'You got shot through the ass! In which case the bullet must've gone right through your brains!' He laughed harshly. 'Goddamn stupid idiot!'

Curly said, 'I'm sorry — '

'Goddamn, useless, good-for-nothing clumsy ox!'

Curly glared at Zeke, who glared back and then laughed. Curly stood a moment, listening to this jeering laughter. He made a sound of anger in his throat, turned and moved away, vanished into the closing darkness.

Zeke said, 'Well, that's torn it!'

* * *

Nino asked, 'You hit, Jesse?'

Jesse was breathing heavily and shaking. He said, 'Don't think so.'

'You were lucky, *hombre*.'

Jesse nodded. 'I'll say. One of 'em gave it away, yelled out, otherwise, I'd've been mutton.'

Nino turned to Paco. 'What if it's Calvin Taylor out there? If it is, will you fight him?'

94

'Sure!'

Jesse said, 'Your mama ain't gonna be too happy, you kill her boyfriend. You lead Taylor to us, Paco?'

Paco turned pale with fear. 'Hell no!'

Jesse put one hand on the grip of his pistol. 'You better not be lying, boy!'

There was one small window in the adobe wall; there was no glass in it, it was covered in a piece of sacking. Nino called through this aperture, 'Taylor? That you out there?'

Taylor's voice came, 'Evening, Henry!'

'How many of you out there?'

'Plenty! And more coming!'

'Hope they're all single men, then.' The Kid laughed. 'Shame to make so many widows and orphans.'

'You worry about your own self. We killed anybody yet?'

Rudabaugh answered. 'Well, Taylor, you didn't kill me, but you got me considerably scared up!'

That brought more laughter, from inside and outside the adobe. Nino asked the outer darkness, 'How you fixed out there?'

'Pretty good. Why'n't you come and join us? Be a little sociable.'

The Kid laughed again. Turning from the window, he began to whistle 'Silver Threads Amongst The Gold' once more.

Dutch Swebke said, 'Looks like they got us treed. What we gonna do?' There was a hint of panic in his voice.

Nino was managing to whistle and grin at the same time. 'Don't worry, Dutch. We got *them* treed, you mean.'

'Come again?'

'I got it all figured out. Soon as it's full dark, me and Jesse'll sneak out. Dig a hole in the corral wall maybe. Get around these fellows and start shooting at them from up above. Nothing so disconcerting to a man sitting out in the dark than finding himself fired at unexpected from behind. While we're distracting 'em, the rest of you boys get on

96

your horses and pile out of the corral.'

Jose Maria Baca said, 'Good plan, Kid. Only when you get out there, behind that posse, you just might forget about coming back and helping us, you might just keep on going!'

Nino slapped the Mexican lightly on the chest. 'Times I think you don't trust me, Jose!'

Jesse said, 'I've got a better plan. One that don't need any shooting. We've got something we can bargain with. Something Taylor'll trade for.'

'What?'

Jesse nodded towards Paco. 'Him.' Jesse drew his pistol and aimed it at Paco's chest; he cocked the weapon. Paco's eyes grew wide with alarm and he backed against the wall. At the same moment, Tom Flynn called, 'Fire!'

9

Zeke Yerby asked, 'How do we play this, Taylor?'

The sheriff didn't answer. He continued to study the adobe through his field glasses. It was dark now, but not full dark as a blue three-quarters moon patched the world. The pattern of shadow and moonlight riffled like black and silver water as wind thrashed the brush.

Zeke said, 'I should've put a bullet in that goddamn Curly. Where is he, anyway?'

O'Keefe asked, 'What happened to that old Navaho?'

'He'll be off somewhere, watching. He'll be enjoying the sight of two lots of white-eyes trying to kill each other.'

Taylor came to a decision. 'Zeke and Pat, you stay here. Stop 'em breaking out of the door. I'll take the rest and cover the corral. Most likely they'll try and break out that way.'

Rhodes said, 'There only seems to be one window they can shoot through. Can't we just rush them?'

'No. You can bet they've knocked loopholes in the walls, so they can cover all sides. All right.' Taylor began to slip off the ridge.

O'Keefe called, 'Look!'

Taylor lifted his head and saw a glimmer of flame in the blue darkness above the adobe, where a ridge shouldered out of the front wall of the mountains. After a second he could make out a dim bulk behind the flame: a man with maybe a lit kerosene lamp in his hand. Someone called, 'That's Curly!'

Curly lobbed the lamp towards the building. It would take a pretty good throw to reach and the lamp fell short. It landed in a clump of mesquite which instantly erupted into yellow flame, pouring oil-black smoke. From inside the adobe a voice yelled, 'Fire!'

Curly lifted to throw again. He ran to the edge of the drop, despite the fact that he was etched clearly against the moonlight. Rifles crashed in the adobe, muzzle flame slanting upwards.

O'Keefe called, 'Curly, you crazy bastard!'

Curly wasn't hit. He threw and ducked back into cover. The lamp caught the corner of the adobe roof and bounced away and fell to earth. A gush of flame broke against the wall, wind fanned it skyward. It lapped around the side of the building and sank back, while a myriad of orange sparks sailed overhead.

Curly ran forward again. Rifles tried for him. Taylor called, 'Cover him!' He jammed the stock of his Winchester into his shoulder, firing at muzzle flash, the others began to fire, too. Curly reached the edge of the drop, threw once more, and the lamp arced through the dark and this time it exploded on the adobe roof. Flames took, the mesquite thatch was instantly ablaze and there were cries of anger and terror from within. Curly froze an instant, clearly visible in the glare of the fire he'd made, staring down, perhaps mesmerized for an instant by his own doings, then he sprang back. And almost made it. Rifles snarled again and caught him half-turning; he staggered and teetered at the edge of the drop and fell.

The dark was suddenly full of the snapping and popping of mesquite as fire took hold of the whole roof. Fanned by the wind it began to roar. For a minute, the possemen watched as the roof burned, as hypnotized as Curly in his fatal moments of hesitation. Taylor felt heat against his face and smoke brought instant tears to his eyes. He came from his dream; he told the others, 'Stay here! Cover the door!' He ran down the wash to where the remaining possemen waited and told them, 'The corral!' He kept running and they followed.

The wash brought the possemen out a hundred yards from the rear of the building, atop a long slope. They flung themselves down in the scant cover there. In the corral, the horses were going crazy. Under the crackling and snarling of the blaze, Taylor heard the screaming of the terrified animals. They milled behind the mesquite bars, streaks of whirling shadow, becoming clearer in the moonlight and the yellow blaze of the roof, rags of fire torn loose and sailing across the sky . . . Taylor glanced behind him, at the faces of the posse limned in flames. They were staring at the adobe, all save Mose Yerby. whose eyes, cold with hatred, were fixed on Taylor . . . then Mose glanced away. Mose's stare put unease in Taylor's stomach, but he forgot it as he slewed back around, watched screaming horses rear against the blaze that had hold of the whole adobe now so that the Regulators had to break clear any minute, or fry. Taylor got his rifle to his shoulder and aimed at the corral, filled with dizziness, terror and exhilaration at the thought of the slaughter that was coming.

Someone flung open the corral gate. Riders reared up against the sky and horses boiled from the corral.

Taylor yelled, 'Take 'em!' He fired low, deliberately, and a horse went down, screaming, thrashing and floundering in the corral entrance. The horses behind veered back, circling, whinnying their terror, pinned against a wall of flame. Then one horseman got his mount under control and urged it forward, yelling. He vaulted his horse over the one on the ground. Horsemen plunged after him.

The posse fired. Their rifles sounded in one continuous blasting. Horses reared against the sky and fell, screaming. A rider fired and Taylor was half-blinded by muzzle-flash. This rider was hit and jerked loose in the saddle; he flopped back against his horse's rump and pitched sideways. Two more riders shot clear of the corral, ducked low against their horses' manes. Taylor fired too fast and missed the first; he tried for the second man and thought he hit; the horsebacker flattened against his mount's neck, then horse and rider were lost in the dark.

Taylor sprang to his feet and plunged down the slope. From the corral there was a blaze of muzzle-flame. Taylor dropped flat, fired at it, then got to his feet and ran downslope again. He found he was yelling like a crazy man. Then a bullet struck the back of his right hip and knocked him forward, turning him; his feet left the earth and he pitched headlong.

He came down on his wounded side. He yelled his pain and kept rolling, then skidded into some rocks which broke his fall and knocked all the wind from him. He lay there for some indeterminate time, trying to breathe. He discovered his rifle was still in his hand; his aching fingers hinged around the lever action.

Slowly, Taylor lifted his head. The

sprawled-out shape of a dead horse blotted the darkness before him. Taylor gazed at it stupidly and a man reared up behind the horse. A black cut-out shape with a pistol in his hand. Taylor dragged his rifle into his shoulder wincing with pain. The man before him fired at the sound. Taylor felt the breath of the bullet on his cheek and hot pain on his neck. He fired. The man was knocked off his feet. He fell sprawling, almost immediately sitting up and Taylor drove another shot into him, knocking him backwards. He rolled twice and then finished up a jackknifed bundle, at the bottom of a slight incline.

Taylor got to his feet. He listened to the silence around him; it rang and echoed in his ears after the madness of gunfire. He felt the sting of blood on the side of his neck where the bullet had nicked him; his side was sodden with blood, soaking his shirt and his right leg. As he took a stumbling step forward blood squeaked in his right boot. He couldn't tell how badly he was hit.

He came to a path of ground that was like a small piece of a battlefield, covered in dead men and horses; almost dead anyway, one horse was still making pathetic attempts to raise its head, whinnying piteously. Taylor paused by the man he'd shot and the man was still alive also. He screamed; Taylor flinched at the sound. The wounded man called, 'They've killed me, boys! Oh Christ!' It was a young, high voice, a voice Taylor knew. Had he got the Kid? *Had he earned his $1,500?*

Other possemen appeared from the gloom around him, swinging kerosene lamps, ghostly figures in the blue moonlight. Taylor counted heads and felt relief when he made it five. He asked, 'Curly?'

O'Keefe shook his head.

'Anybody else hurt?'

It turned out that Taylor was the only one who'd been hit. His side hurt like fire, but he'd already decided that, for all the blood, his wound wasn't serious; the bullet had only grazed him.

The possemen started tidying up, someone shot the dying horse. Two dead men were dragged from the shadows and laid out in the moonlight where they could be seen.

Dutch Swebke and Jose Maria Baca.

Taylor's victim screamed again and someone leaned over him with a lamp. Taylor recognized Red Tom Flynn. Like the other two Regulators, he was fairly riddled with bullets. The boy began to cry out for his mother and then the crying stopped abruptly.

Rhodes stared down. He said, 'He's nothing but a boy.'

Taylor nodded, scowling. 'Seventeen years old.'

The rattle started in the boy's throat; the possemen stopped what they were doing to listen — except Sam Yerby, he was still poking through the carnage. Then he paused and laughed. He said,

'Well, looky here!'

Possemen walked over to him. He was staring down, his shotgun rested across his arms. There was a dead horse at his feet, and a man pinned under it by the leg. The man was pressed flat on his face to the sand, his arms stretched out before him. A pistol lay just beyond the reach of his right hand, a Colt .41 double action. For a moment, as the posse gathered around him, he lay still, then he raised his head. He said, 'Hello, Taylor.'

'Hello, Kid.'

Nino glanced over at his pistol and Sam Yerby said, 'What's the matter? Can't you reach?' He kicked the pistol and it skittered across the sand towards the Kid's hand.

O'Keefe said, 'You crazy bastard!'

Sam grinned and lifted his shotgun. 'Let him try for it.'

Taylor reached down and grabbed the pistol.

Sam asked, 'What's the matter? You begrudge me the reward?' He gestured with the two black mouths of his shotgun. It was an American Army 12 gauge, its barrel sawn down to widen the blast-pattern at short range. 'Five hundred dollars for the man gets this little bastard!'

'Money we're *all* gonna share. And on the others too. We all risked our necks; we each get a cut.'

O'Keefe said, 'Yeah, wasn't just you here, Sam!'

Sam glared. Taylor felt a surge of temper. 'Do I have to fight all of you goddamn Yerbys?'

The Kid was dragged from under his horse. He sat, kneading his leg. 'You killed my bay mare, Taylor.'

'Good horse you stole there.'

Taylor searched the Kid, finding a knife. Then he clipped handcuffs around the prisoner's wrists. He told Nino, 'You got thin wrists, but you ain't gonna slip these irons.'

'You just made history, Taylor. You're the first person ever put the bracelets on me.' The Kid lifted his wrists and eyed his manacles with distaste. 'The others?'

'We killed Dutch, Jose and Tom.'

'Tom.' Nino shook his head.

'Just about wiped out you Regulators. Jesse got away. And another one. I think maybe I hit him.'

O'Keefe said, 'He looked like a Mexican.'

Taylor asked, 'Who was it, Kid?'

The Kid grinned. For an instant there was a look on his face that Taylor didn't understand. He began to say something, then changed it to; 'Find out.'

Taylor felt a strange unease a moment. It passed. 'Another damn fool you got to come along with you. Even though they know how they'll end up. Like you're going to end up.'

'And how's that?'

'On the end of a rope.'

'Nobody's going to hang me.'

'No?'

'Sam'd like to do it. Wouldn't you, Sam?' The Kid laughed. 'You'd like to yank the rope your own self after I marked your face up!'

Sam lifted his shotgun and lunged towards the prisoner. Taylor came between them. He pushed Sam back. Taylor said, 'Hold it, Sam! This man's going to hang! He's going to dangle where everyone can see him. Nothing else is going to happen to him! You hear?'

Sam glared some more. Then he spat on the earth and walked away.

Taylor told the others, 'All right. We're pulling out. 'Less you want to be waiting here when Jesse Rudabaugh gets back with some of his friends.'

The gathering broke up. As Taylor walked off, he felt a stab of pain behind his right hip, he halted and put his hand to the wound. As Mose Yerby stepped past him, Taylor said, 'Funny thing about this nick. Feels like the bullet hit me from *behind*. Yet the Regulators was all in front of us.'

Mose paused. 'Must've been a ricochet. Or maybe an accidental shot.'

He smiled. 'Accidents can happen to anybody.'

Taylor gazed at the other man a moment. 'That's right. 'Specially around here. They used to call travelling through this country the *jornado del muerto* — the journey of death — did you know that, Mose?' When Mose nodded, Taylor went on, 'And like you said, accidents can happen to anybody.'

Taylor became conscious he'd rested his left hand on his pistol in its cross-draw holster; Mose's hands were hitched around his belt, as far away from the grip of his pistol as he could put them.

For another minute the two men studied each other. Then, still smiling, Mose walked away.

The Kid approached, with O'Keefe following, his rifle in his hands. The prisoner was whistling jauntily. O'Keefe observed. 'You're pretty cheerful.'

'I'm lucky. All that flying lead, I never got so much as a crease.'

'Lucky are you?'

Taylor asked, 'Any last words for your friends back there?'

Nino considered a moment. 'Tom was too young for this game. The others — ' He shrugged. 'They took their chances. I'm beholden, Taylor — you kept Sam from putting a bullet in me back there. First time I was ever saved by the law.'

Taylor glanced at the Kid and remembered they'd once been friends; then he remembered the badge on his shirt. 'No bullet for you.'

'No?'

'I'm saving you to hang.'

The Kid kept grinning, but all the friendliness flickered out of his eyes. He said, 'You'll play the devil getting it done, Taylor.'

10

The following article appeared in the *Oxford County Chronicle:*

The notorious outlaw Henry McCarthy was found guilty today of the first degree murder of Azariah F. Kelly, former sheriff of Oxford County ... the judge directed that the said prisoner be turned over to the present sheriff of Oxford County to be confined in jail in Oxford until Friday, 14 September 1881. And on that day, between the hours of nine and three, the said Henry McCarthy, alias The Arizona Kid, alias Kid McCarthy etc., is to be hanged by the neck until his body be dead ...

A ragged calender hung lopsidedly on the otherwise bare adobe wall of the

Oxford jailhouse. It said 28 August.

The Arizona Kid was finishing lunch. He'd been let out of his cell to eat with his jailers. He and they had a little competition going: who could bite deepest into a pie. It was a competition the Kid, with his two squirrel-like front teeth, won easily, to laughter. The only person not laughing was Sam Yerby. The deputy leaned against the wall on the far side of the room. He was loading eighteen buckshot into each barrel of his shotgun.

His mouth full of pie, the Kid said, 'Careful you don't shoot yourself, Sam.'

Sam patted the barrel of his gun. 'The man gets one of these loads'll feel it.'

The Kid belched, which was a compliment for good cooking in this country, and rocked back in his chair. O'Keefe said, 'You seem to be taking this pretty easy.'

'What's the point of looking on the gloomy side of things?'

Taylor said, 'I hear you killed your first man when you was only twelve.'

'Heard that too. No, boys, my first crime was at the tender age of fifteen. I got into bad company and that led me into my first brush with the law. On a bet, I stole some clothes out of a Chinee laundry. Got me my first spell of incarceration then. A night in jail, only I skinned out: climbed out up the chimney.'

O'Keefe and Taylor laughed. Sam got to his feet, scowling. He told the other lawmen, 'You two, acting like he's your friend or something. Like he's just some wild boy gone wrong. Curly's dead, isn't he? Maybe this one did it.'

O'Keefe said, 'Ease off, Sam. The Kid'll answer soon enough.'

'Not soon enough for me!'

The Irishman grinned. 'Sam's just sorry you never made a break for it, Kid, so he can try out his nice new toy.'

Sam's face darkened. He seemed

116

to be looking for words a moment; he gave that up and spat on the earth floor.

The Kid said, 'Pity your mama never got round to learning you Yerbys any manners. Still, where you was raised, way back in the sticks, what can you expect?'

Sam took a step towards the prisoner. Taylor said, 'Sam, why the hell you keep letting him ride you? Maybe you better just get some air.'

Yerby stepped towards the door. Before he left, he told the Kid, 'You'll be swinging like a piece of meat out in that plaza, while the women and kids are all laughing at you. I'll be laughing too. Watching you kick. You ever see a hanging? Face turns red, then purple, then black; tongue sticks out, you piss all over . . . '

The sheriff told the prisoner, 'Back in the cell, Kid.'

After O'Keefe had locked Nino in his cell on the first floor of the building, Taylor and the deputy went out on the balcony there, overlooking the main Oxford plaza. O'Keefe leaned on the balcony rail. He said, 'You know what fear smells of? Sulphur. I've got the smell of it on me, waiting to get it over with. Nino's the only one who doesn't seem to be sweating.'

Taylor nodded. 'That's what's bothering me. Don't get too easy with him, Pat.'

'You were laughing with him just now.'

'Sure. But that's the Kid for you — laughing, friendly as all hell, but he'd kill you pretty quick if he could. He's just watching for you or Sam to get careless. And it's like you said, he isn't sweating and he ought to be.'

'You think the other Regulators might try and spring him?'

'What other Regulators? All that's left is Jesse Rudabaugh and whoever was with him at Bad Water.'

'He's still got friends amongst the Mexicans.'

Taylor frowned, thinking about that. 'Yeah.'

Sam reappeared. He climbed the wooden steps to the first floor. 'Somebody wants to see you Taylor, over by the old church.'

Taylor raised an eyebrow. 'Who?'

Yerby shrugged. 'Somebody.' His lips twisted with disdain and Taylor knew who was waiting for him. All three men went down the stairs to the main office. The sheriff said, 'Both of you stay here 'til I get back.'

Sam sank into a chair and fanned his face with his hat. 'You've told us: two men with the Kid at all times.' He laid his shotgun on the improvised desk, one hand resting on the finely engraved faceplate. 'Why? He ain't going nowhere.'

Taylor said, 'I won't be long.' He left.

Sam grinned at O'Keefe. 'Taylor's off to see his greaser whore.'

O'Keefe took a thread of tobacco from his bottom lip. 'Someday soon,

119

someone's going to kill you, Sam.'

Yerby laughed.

★ ★ ★

Taylor met Pilar in a grove of big pepper trees by the walls of the old Spanish church. They spent a minute in silence while he gazed at Pilar and she tried not to look at him.

Pilar said, 'It's about Paco. When you came back . . . from the White Sands . . . well, Paco was gone for a week.'

'The hell with Paco! He's old enough to shift for himself. What I'm concerned about is you and me.'

Pilar glared. 'You would say that. When he got back, his horse was run almost to death. There was a bullet scar on the saddle. Paco had a scar, too, right across his back. He wouldn't let me see, but I saw his shirt where the bullet had torn it. And then I saw where he'd been wounded.' She had Taylor's attention now. 'And the dust

120

on his horse. Lot of dust, hard to swab out. White dust.'

'Gypsum? Like in the White Sands?'

Pilar didn't answer that. Taylor asked, 'You figure he was running with the Kid? If he was with the Kid, out at Dirty Springs, then maybe I gave him that bullet scar.' He sat on the edge of the ruined fountain, resting his fist against his mouth. After a time, he asked, 'Where's Paco now?'

'I didn't tell you all so you could kill him! I thought maybe you'd forget you were the sheriff for a minute and think of me. And Paco. But I was the one who forgot. There's a reward for the men who killed Curly. That's all you think about now, isn't it?'

He stood. Pilar said, 'Money, Taylor!' She almost spat out the words. 'All you have to do is kill another Mexican!'

Taylor began to walk back towards the jail, changed his mind and went into the Mexican part of town looking for Paco. He spent half an hour looking. Finally he located Paco's horse out front of a *tendejon*, a shop that also doubled as a saloon. He inspected the animal, noting the long gouge in the saddle. Then he lifted the animal's hooves and bent to inspect them, one by one. Under the horse's belly, he saw approaching feet. He straightened up so that the horse was between him and this newcomer: it was Paco.

The boy halted and stared at him. Taylor stared too. It wasn't a boy Taylor faced, but a man, dressed like a well-to-do *charro*, in narrow leather pants, short, winged leather jacket, decorated with arabesques of braid and steeple-crowned sombrero. A handsome young man any mother would be proud of and any young woman might smile at. There ought to be a gun about him, but Taylor couldn't see one.

The sheriff said, 'Well, Paco, you look quite the gentleman. You going somewhere?'

'What you want with my horse?'

'I see the near front hoof is split.'

'That don't prove anything!'

'You know what it proves and so do I.'

Paco ran his tongue between his lips. Now he had a trapped look about him, like a dangerous young animal. His hands moved as if seeking the gun that wasn't there. Taylor said, 'You know now what happens to everybody runs with the Kid. He walks away and they end up in the ground. You want to end up the same way? Hasn't your mother lost enough, what with your pa — '

'Don't you talk about him!'

Taylor stepped around the horse. Paco retreated several paces. He said, 'You're going to whip me? *You're* not my father!'

'I'm not going to whip you. That's how I'd treat a kid, and you ain't one no more.'

Paco looked almost pleased at that; then the trapped, dangerous look came back to his face. 'So, treat me like a man. Kill me like one!'

The sheriff shook his head. 'I'm

trying to keep you alive, Paco. You think you're the Kid's friend? He doesn't have any. Just people around him who get between him and the next bullet — '

Taylor broke off then, there was a burst of gunfire. It came from the town behind him, perhaps half a mile distant: from the direction of the jail.

Taylor turned towards the firing. He lifted his pistol from its scabbard. Something slammed into his back and knocked him forward and he ploughed to his knees. The gun fell from his hand. He grabbed for it, dimly aware that Paco had rammed into his back, was looming above him. The boy threw a handful of fine sand into Taylor's eyes. Taylor cried out, blinded. As he blinked to clear his eyes, he saw Paco had snatched up the pistol, was turning it towards him.

Paco cried, 'Don't, Taylor!' his voice high with fear. Taylor grabbed the boy's wrist, they struggled to turn the pistol this way and that.

Taylor cried, 'Don't be a damn fool, Paco!'

The black mouth of the pistol was pointed at Taylor, then at Paco, then straight up into the air between them. The gun went off. The muzzle was only inches from Taylor's eyes; there was an explosion of fire that filled his vision, that burst like shrapnel in his head. An explosion without sound. Taylor was falling, he was conscious of that much; then there was only darkness.

11

Sam Yerby said, 'My belly feels like my throat's been cut. Where's Taylor?'

O'Keefe didn't reply. He tilted his long frame back in his chair and gazed at the ceiling, his hands cupped behind his head.

Sam said, 'I'm going to get some lunch.'

'You know what Taylor said — two of us with the Kid at all times.'

Sam sneered, 'Where the hell is Taylor anyway? I'll tell you where — he's making up for lost time with that Pilar.' Sam ran a thumb down his cheek scar. 'She is a looker, mind, if you don't mind dark meat . . . '

O'Keefe gazed at Yerby with distaste.

From the cell upstairs, the Kid called, 'I want to go.'

Sam said, 'Piss yourself!' He began to chuckle at his own wit.

O'Keefe got to his feet reluctantly. After a moment, Sam rose also, grumbling. The deputies climbed the stairs to the cell. The prisoner sat on the edge of his bed, shackled hand and foot. While Sam watched, his shotgun in his hands, O'Keefe unlocked the cell door. All three men descended the steps with O'Keefe ahead of the prisoner and Sam behind him. As the Kid neared the bottom step, Sam swung out with the barrel of his shotgun. He caught the prisoner just above the right hip, the Kid tumbled down the last few steps and ended up sprawled on all fours.

Sam said, 'Careful of the stairs there.' He chuckled.

Nino got to his feet, slowly. He winced with pain, lifted his manacled hands and tried to rub his back. O'Keefe glowered at Yerby, but the Kid was still smiling. He said, 'You look like you're busting to say something, Sam.'

Yerby grinned. 'The great Arizona Kid, kicking on a rope . . . That's no way for a dog to die. Not even you.'

'No?'

Yerby studied the sawn-off in his hands. 'If you want, I could make it easy for you . . . Why don't you make a run for it?'

'No thanks.' Still smiling, the Kid stepped out through the doorway.

* * *

He was smiling because it was time. The day had come. He'd been waiting for the signal, counting off the days and hours as they shrank away, thinking of the rope and kicking and twisting on the end of it, the long dying as he strangled . . . and then, today, the signal had come. He'd seen Paco in the smaller plaza behind the jailhouse and that had been the signal. It meant Jesse Rudabaugh was round here somewhere and everything was set. It would all go sweet providing his luck, which had always held, held once more . . . and provided he kept his nerve, like he always had.

Nino set off across the plaza, O'Keefe following. The prisoner hopped and hobbled to the tiny adobe hut that passed for a privy, a narrow, foul-smelling, fly-buzzing *jacal* he could barely stand in, let alone a taller man. O'Keefe looked in first, stooped over, glanced about. There was a bad moment when he paused and stared at the wall. The Kid waited. But O'Keefe seemed satisfied; he stepped outside and the Kid entered. He sat and O'Keefe pushed the steerhide door to. Nino sighed with relief. Very quietly he moved from the seat and squatted down against the wall, tapping the adobe until there was a hollow sound under his knuckles. He could see pale scars where the adobe had been cut with a knife. He gripped the wall and a section of plaster came away in his hand. There it was, in a cavity in the wall. A drawstring leather bag. Nino removed the bag and opened it. Inside was a Colt-Frontier double-action .45, with six bullets in the chamber.

Breath caught in Nino's throat. He felt almost dizzy, admiring the beauty of the weapon, its power. This small, chunky wedge of dark metal changed everything. He was no longer an animal in a cage waiting for a slow, strangling death, something for fools to ogle and laugh at. He was once again in charge of events. All he had to do was keep his nerve and wait just a little longer . . . go back to the jail, get the drop on the deputies and get free of these irons, then tie his former guards and run for it.

Nino's wrists were trembling. He felt dazed with fear. Now, if ever, he needed to hold steady . . .

Pat kicked the door. The Kid said, 'I'm coming, you long-legged son of a bitch!' and the other man laughed. Nino stuffed the gun under his shirt and left the outhouse. He shambled along ahead of O'Keefe who was smiling at his own thoughts. The prisoner frowned, he hoped O'Keefe wouldn't try anything. Let him remember the pittance the county paid him as a deputy and not act like a hero! He liked the Irishman, but he'd kill him if he had to. As for Sam Yerby . . . he could still feel the sharp pain in his back where Yerby had struck him. It would be so pleasant to kill Sam, especially with his own shotgun. Let him have two barrels of his own buckshot . . . It was a mouth-watering prospect.

Still, it would be more sensible to make his escape quietly, without guns going off. But the Kid knew how hard it would be to stop from killing Sam once he had the chance . . . already he felt a strange energy trembling through him. It seemed to ripple out from the grip of the hidden gun. He felt it in the dryness of his mouth, the palms of his hands. Maybe he could find a knife somewhere and settle Yerby that way.

Prisoner and deputy entered the jail. O'Keefe called, 'Sam!' a few times, but the building was empty.

The Kid noted Sam's shotgun racked with the other guns along the wall. He said, 'Looks like Sam's gone to lunch after all.' He heard fear in his voice.

O'Keefe didn't seem to notice that; he just grunted in answer and reached for the cell keys on the crate that passed for a desk.

Sam disobeying Taylor's orders and leaving the Kid just one man to deal with! Nino's luck was holding all right; it was getting better! Now, if only Taylor stayed away awhile longer, and Pat didn't play the fool . . .

O'Keefe's back was momentarily turned to the prisoner; while it was, the Kid produced the gun from under his shirt. O'Keefe turned and the Kid jammed the barrel of the pistol in his ribs.

O'Keefe turned pale. 'Don't be crazy, Kid!'

'You worry about your own self! Get these bracelets off me!'

O'Keefe gaped. Nino drove the gun barrel harder into the other's side. 'Do it, Pat! I don't want to kill you, but I will, by God!'

The Irishman stood frozen. The Kid worked back the hammer of the double-action, noticing how heavy the trigger pull was, especially as his hands had become slow and out of practice with guns. But the hard click of metal decided O'Keefe, who threw his pistol into a corner of the room and found the handcuff keys. He unlocked the irons around Nino's wrists and dropped them on the floor. Then he crouched down and unlocked the fetters around Nino's ankles.

The Kid said, 'Good! Now — '

O'Keefe swung the leg irons. One clamp and a length of chain caught the Kid against the side of the face, knocking him half around. He tumbled backwards over the desk. As he struck the earth, O'Keefe kicked the crate and it upended on the Kid. Nino got a foot against the crate and pushed it away; O'Keefe paused, deciding whether to dive after his pistol or make a break for the door. He chose the latter. As he lunged for the doorway, Nino fired. The trigger pull threw him; he missed. He fired again. Dust spumed from the wall, then O'Keefe flung the door wide and plunged outside. He ran into the plaza.

The Kid stared after him. His luck was out after all, he'd missed twice at next-to-nothing range. He was going to finish here . . . but at least he'd die with a gun in his hand. Not kicking and choking on a rope.

Then he saw O'Keefe was moving strangely.

The deputy was slowing, his knees bending, following a weaving path. He sank to his knees, twisted, then sprawled on his back. He lifted his knees into his body. His hands were clutching his side. Nino saw there was blood all over the Irishman's shirt and pants. O'Keefe was moaning softly, 'Oh God . . . oh God . . . oh God!' The shot that had gone into the wall . . . the Kid had caught O'Keefe in the guts with a ricochet!

For a moment, seeing O'Keefe writhing in his blood, moaning his agony, the Kid felt horror, revulsion at what he'd done. But he snapped out of that in an instant. He was calm once more, in control again . . . Any minute Sam and Taylor would come running, best for the Kid to bolt now.

But he didn't. He ran back upstairs. He opened the door to the balcony and waited there, crouched down against the door jamb, staring through the slits in the balcony railings. After a minute he heard running feet. Sam Yerby came across the plaza at a jog. He halted when he saw O'Keefe, twisting against the earth in a spreading lake of his own blood. Sam stared, the look on his face almost comic. Then he came out of his reverie and turned and looked across the plaza, the way the Kid might have run. Then another thought struck him and Nino saw Yerby's face change, he turned his head and gazed at the jailhouse, thinking, What if the prisoner hadn't run? What if he was still in the jail?

Nino smiled. He said, 'Up here, Sam.'

Sam lifted his head and saw the Kid, because Nino had moved from his crouched position in the doorway and stood on the balcony in full view. His elbows rested on the rail. Sam's American Arms shotgun was in his hands, the great black eyes of the barrel stared into Sam's eyes.

For a moment Sam stood helplessly. Then he seemed to remember the pistol in his holster. He grabbed for it, opening his mouth to cry out. The shotgun spoke first. It made a thunder that rocked the whole plaza. The Kid fired the lefthand barrel; eighteen grains of buckshot took Sam in the face. He was flung backwards like a toy, twisted in the air and came down on his front. He rested his face on the sand. Except now he had no face.

The Kid watched Sam kick. He

laughed. He decided Yerby was too long dying so he took careful aim and let the deputy have the other barrel in the back and the back of the head. The Kid found he was whooping and laughing, jumping up and down on the balcony like an excited child. It was some time before he got hold of himself and remembered Taylor and began to think of escape.

O'Keefe was still making whimpering noises, although the sounds were feebler now. Nino felt regret, looking down on the Irishman. But gazing at the bloody corpse of Sam Yerby, he started to laugh again. He flung the shotgun down and it struck the dead man across the legs. The Kid called, 'Here's your gun back, Sam! You won't follow me with it no more, damn you!'

12

Taylor's eyes were open, but he couldn't see. The world before him was dim and yellowy, like he was staring through a gauzy bandage. He lifted a hand to his face and found he *was* bandaged across his eyes. He started to lift the thick rag.

A voice was speaking. Taylor recognized Emmet Rhodes' voice. The newspaperman said, 'The doctor doesn't know how badly your eyes are damaged. You're to keep that bandage on — ' but by that time, Taylor had raised the binding over his eyes.

Pilar said, 'Damn you, Taylor.'

Harsh light came like little sharp knives into his eyes and he cried out in pain. He blinked and his eyes watered. All that was before him was a yellow glare, scouring his eyeballs. He felt terror then, he thought: Paco's blinded me. Then wavering streaks came into the yellow swimming like tadpoles. These streaks thickened, gained colour, suddenly he could see the faces, the people around him. He managed to sit up, although an axe blade of pain threatened to crack his head open. At the same time he let out a long sigh of relief that at least he wasn't blind.

He saw he was in an unfamiliar room, laid out on a table. There were two more tables and a man laid out on each of them also. The coroner's office? The doctor's? Then he remembered that in Oxford the coroner and doctor were one and the same.

The doctor wasn't in the room, just Rhodes, ashen-faced. And Pilar sitting in a chair, she appeared to be weeping.

Taylor swung about, bringing his feet down to earth; the pain in his head was so bad he thought he was going to faint; then the world steadied about him. Rhodes said, 'You really should keep your eyes bandaged.'

Taylor saw the man on the table next to him was covered in a blanket. Taylor pulled it back. He had a strong-enough stomach and he'd seen plenty of corpses in his time; for all that he gasped, looking down. From his size and clothes the dead man was Sam Yerby, his face wiped away by buckshot. Taylor dropped the blanket back over the corpse. Pat O'Keefe lay, groaning, on the next table. O'Keefe had been shot in the side and there was blood all over him. His face was grey with shock and the nearness of his death. Taylor said, 'Oh Christ, Pat.'

The Irishman's lips twisted into a grotesque approximation of a smile. He spent a moment trying to speak. Finally he managed to say, 'I thought I had a chance until I saw the look on your face then.'

'I'm sorry, Pat.'

'Wasn't your fault.'

Taylor gazed at Rhodes. 'I suppose the Kid is long gone.'

Rhodes nodded. 'He took his time. After he shot Sam he spent five minutes laughing and dancing around on the balcony. In full view of everybody. You think he's gone crazy?'

'Guns make people crazy. Anybody know how he managed it — escaping?'

O'Keefe lifted his head slightly. 'The Kid got hold of — '

'Don't talk.'

But O'Keefe persisted. He managed to say, 'Got hold of a pistol. I reckon it was hidden in the privy. I searched in there before, but it was hidden somewhere I didn't see.'

Zeke Yerby said, 'Yeah, one of his greaser friends hid it there!'

Taylor lifted his head and saw Zeke and Mose Yerby in the doorway. The sheriff said, 'I'm sorry about Sam.'

Mose turned his anguished face towards Taylor. 'You are a goddamn liar!'

Zeke studied O'Keefe. 'How is it, Irish?'

'My luck was out. That he hit me

141

at all was a scratch — got me with a ricochet.'

Zeke nodded, grim-faced. 'That's too bad,' he said, without sarcasm.

Mose declared, 'Now it's your turn to take your medicine.' Seeing the look Taylor gave him, Mose said, 'Well, you're not so big now, are you, Mister Sheriff? You was a big man all right, wiping out the Kid's gang, capturing him. Biggest man in this territory. But now you're pretty small, letting him get away. Maybe you was even in on it yourself!'

'Come again?'

'It's my guess it was Paco stashed that gun in the outhouse.' Mose glared at Pilar with hatred. 'Your greaser whore's kid!'

'Mose!'

Mose took a step towards the lawman; Zeke placed a hand on his arm. 'This isn't the place for a quarrel.'

Rhodes said, 'That's right! We have an injured man here.'

Zeke said, 'We came here to collect our kin. For burying. That's all.'

There was a thick silence. Taylor broke it, saying, 'I can still use you as deputies.'

Zeke shook his head. 'No, we've finished with your rules now. Your kind of law. We'll find the Kid and settle him, like you should've done. Only we'll do it *our* way.'

The Yerbys took their dead brother between them, wrapped in the blanket, and carried him from the office. Taylor sat in a chair. A regular war was going on in his head, cannon fire thudding against his temples. He pressed his hands against them. O'Keefe said, 'Well, you warned us. Me and Sam.'

'Wasn't your fault.'

Taylor asked Pilar, 'Where's Paco, Pilar? Did he ride out with the Kid?'

Her face twisted with grief, taking away all her beauty. Taylor was almost shocked, seeing that. 'You want me to tell you where he is, so you can kill him?'

'Like I told Paco — I want to keep him alive.'

'What? So you can hang him instead of shooting him?'

'Where'd he go, Pilar?'

She didn't answer. Rhodes asked Taylor, 'So I suppose you're going out after Nino?'

Pilar said, 'Maybe he'll run off to Mexico.'

'If he has any sense he will. But . . . '

'You could let him go!'

Taylor thought about it a moment, then he shook his head slowly. 'No. He's got to be stopped. Everything he touches . . . everyone who's with him . . . Look what he's brought here.'

O'Keefe said, 'Like they say in the old country: he's one born for sorrow.' O'Keefe became quiet again. The others listened to his breathing. Then he announced, 'Paco was always a good kid. Good man, like his pa.' He took a short, snatched breath, then another one; then no more.

13

The last of the Regulators lay about in a rock house, an abandoned way station for cattle drivers and sheep herders, the bare shell of a house with no door in the doorway or glass in the windows, so that dust sifted through, the wind outside making discordant organ noises. Inside, the Arizona Kid sat against the wall in a corner of the one room, laughing as he read aloud from a dime novel: 'The notorious bandit the Arizona Kid wore drawers of fine scarlet broadcloth and a beaver hat covered in gold and jewels . . . This bloodthirsty young desperado, who had a heart only for anatomical purposes . . . ' The Kid broke off his reading to ask, 'What's the matter, Paco?'

Paco stared at the earth. The boy had barely spoken at all in the last few days.

Jesse Rudabaugh was cleaning his rifle. 'He's still thinking about O'Keefe and Sam.'

The Kid sighed. 'You know I didn't want to kill O'Keefe, Paco! How many times have I got to say it? I *liked* Pat. But . . . '

Jesse spat on an oiling rag. 'We're crazy, hanging around here. Soon as you busted loose, we should've run straight for Mexico.'

'What, and let Taylor run us out?'

'A sensible man runs away to fight another day. While he can.'

The Kid began whistling, an old dance tune named 'Turkey in the Straw.'

Jesse frowned. 'You got too famous, busting out of jail like that. You're about the most famous outlaw in the whole country now!'

The Kid lifted the dime novel. 'Leader of two, three hundred desperadoes it says here!'

'You still thinking about Celsa? Plenty more like her down in old

Mex. Anyway, you could send for her, once we're across the line. If she loves you, she'll follow you anywhere.'

Nino smiled. 'They all love me, Jesse.'

That brought more silence, back-clothed by the low, keening wind. Then Jesse asked, 'What *are* we going to do? All the waterholes north and east of here got posses sitting on 'em. They're coming all around us, Henry. Like a trap closing.'

'They're north and east, we go south and west.'

'Mean country that way. The White Sands, the *jornado del muerto*, the mountains — '

Another silence, save for the bleary sawing of the wind. Suddenly, Jesse lifted a rock and flung it at Paco; it skinned flesh from his right shin. Paco didn't respond; instead he pulled his knees into his body and hunched forward. He ducked his head between his knees and began to rock. Jesse got to his feet. 'Goddamn you, Paco! Why don't you say something?'

Nino said, 'Leave the boy alone.'

'Sitting there! Why don't you just run home to your mama? All you are is bad luck waiting to happen.' Jesse glared at Paco, his face dark with anger, he already had his hand on the grip of his pistol.

Nino said, 'All right, Jesse.'

The Arizona Kid stood also. For a moment, Jesse had the bizarre thought that the Kid was going to make a play for his own gun, that the two of them were going to have it out, here and now. Instead, the younger man said, 'Maybe you're right.'

'About what?'

'Maybe we should try Mexico.'

Jesse sighed; he was surprised at the relief he felt. 'Now you're talking sense, Henry.'

'First water south of here is at Deer Creek. After that, it's only three days to Mexico.'

Jesse walked out of the building. Nino tapped Paco on the shoulder.

He said, 'Come on, kid! Time to rattle hocks. You ever been to the old country?'

Paco lifted his head. His face was a child's, twisted in misery; his eyes were red with tears.

★ ★ ★

The Regulators approached Deer Creek from the north, through a belt of bare, stony hills that reflected the sun's heat like buckled tin. They paused there, in cover, while Jesse scanned the waterhole with his field glasses. He said, 'Damn!'

Nino pulled off his faded bandanna and used it to scour some of the sweat and salt dust out of his neck and face. 'What?'

'Three . . . no, four of them.'

Paco was shading up under the belly of his horse, taking refuge from the blinding, metallic light. His voice rasping from thirst, he said, 'Taylor must have men sitting on every waterhole in this country.'

Jesse said, 'I guess he wants you real bad, Paco.'

The Kid grinned. 'It's not Paco he's after. Like you said, Jesse, I got to be too famous, busting jail and all!'

Jesse blinked sweat out of his eyes and squinted against the sun's glare. 'Well, what now? We give it up?'

The Kid fanned his face with his battered sombrero. 'I'm not anxious to feel a rope around my neck. I could feel it there before . . . tightening. While I was sitting in that jail. Not again.'

'What then?'

Nino turned his head and gazed westward. Beyond the desert were the mountains. Seen through haze they were soft images that rippled under the blue sheet of the sky; in reality they were jagged and naked, the cruel ramparts of a dead world. Nino moved his tongue around in his mouth to find the moisture to speak. 'Dead Man's Wells usually has water in it.'

'Let's hope so. Otherwise these

horses'll die under us, then where are we?'

For once, the Kid didn't find a joke to answer with; he just kneed his tired horse into motion, riding towards the west. Slowly, his companions followed.

Nino was right. There *was* water at Dead Man's Well. Emmet Rhodes and Calvin Taylor were there too.

★ ★ ★

There was a full moon that night, turning the desert pale blue, but, unusually, cloud scudded over the moon's face. The sky was eerily light but the land was murky, blotched with shadow. A chill wind combed the earth, swaying the few gnarled mesquites and cottonwoods that grew about Dead Man's Wells.

The two men were in the rocks and trees over-looking the waterhole. Both had rifles at their sides. Taylor blew on his hands, rubbed them together. He decided that, of all things, he hated cold most. He asked Rhodes, 'Who'll run your newspaper while you're out here?'

'It'll keep. I had to do this. For Pat.'

Taylor nodded, frowning. 'We'll get them. Nobody gives a damn about the Yerbys, but the Kid killing Pat . . . that's turned this whole country against him. Even some of the Mexicans. There's posses out of Texas, ranchers from over there guarding all the waterholes north and east of here. We've got men between him and the border. So he'll have to come this way. Only we're getting men up here too.'

'And Paco?'

Taylor grunted and began to reply, then he heard, ringingly loud in the cathedral silence of the night, the whinny of a horse.

Sound could travel a long way through this darkness. Taylor squinted through the moonlight and saw nothing. When Rhodes began to speak, Taylor gave him a sharp look and the newspaperman held his tongue. The sheriff took his rifle and sank into cover behind a fair-sized boulder, Rhodes took cover behind another large rock.

The two men waited in silence, then more faint sounds pushed into this void, the sounds of men and horses in motion. Out of the shadow-patched blueness of the desert floor came a moving shadow: three riders bunched together. Taylor laid his Winchester across the top of the boulder, eared back the hammer. His mouth was hot and dry with fear. In his imagination he was looking along the barrel of the rifle and there was a face framed in the sights.

Paco's face.

Rhodes whispered, 'How do we know it's them?'

Out of the side of his mouth, Taylor said, 'Wait and see. Don't shoot 'til I do.'

The bunched horsemen came to a place where the trail narrowed between rocks. To pass through they moved into single file. Taylor studied the dim shape of the leading rider until his tired eyes ached. The shape of the man's hat, the tilt at which he wore it, the easy way he rode, was it the Kid? If only the moon would shake free of the clouds, then he could see!

The newcomers came from the shadows of the rocks, strung out. The leader was well ahead of his companions now. Taylor had the man's chest fixed in the front sight of his Winchester and he was almost certain it was Nino. Fear had spread from Taylor's throat, cold and rotten as hunger in his belly; there was a dizziness in his head, a humming in his ears, a faint trembling in his arms and legs . . . His finger eased against the trigger, began to pull . . .

Suddenly the nearest horseman veered his horse aside and rode back, past the middle rider, approaching the man bringing up the rear. At the same time, the moon shook free of cloud and the desert was a checkerboard, quarters of blue light and darkness. Taylor glimpsed the face of the nearest rider, the man who'd been in the middle of the file a minute ago: it was Jesse Rudabaugh.

As under his breath as he could the sheriff told Rhodes, 'It's them.'

The rearmost riders held their horses still. Taylor thought he heard the murmur of voices. Jesse came on. Taylor felt relief that it wasn't Paco, relief that quickly turned to meanness, to anger. A killing would let out that anger . . . he had his sights fixed on Jesse's chest as the horseman loomed larger, he only had to squeeze . . . He thought, that's it. Keep coming. Just a little closer, you son of a bitch!

Jesse must have heard or sensed something. Suddenly, he swung his horse aside. His rifle came into his hand. He shouted, 'Kid!'

Taylor surprised himself too. He called, 'Hold it!' Jesse fired at the sound, the muzzle flash blinding Taylor, who fired and missed. Jesse's horse reared and plunged, spinning about.

Taylor could see again, fired and missed once more. Jesse spurred his horse into movement and was hit by Rhodes' shot. He pitched from the saddle.

The two most distant riders produced guns and fired. Taylor and Rhodes turned their rifles on them, Taylor pumping the Winchester lever like a crazy man. He had halfway emptied the magazine before it came to him he was shooting at Paco. The two horsemen scattered into the dark.

Rhodes lifted from cover, took a step towards the fallen man. Taylor began to yell a warning as Jesse fired from the ground. Rhodes grunted and went down. Jesse rolled to his knees. The Winchester kicked against Taylor's shoulder and the outlaw was knocked backwards.

Taylor called, 'Rhodes!'

Rhodes was sitting up, clutching his right leg with both hands.

Jesse pushed himself upright. He lifted his pistol once more. Taylor snap-aimed, fired, and saw Jesse jerk to the bullet, spinning half about. From the earth, Rhodes got a hand to his own pistol, drew it and fired. Both possemen fired again; only then did Jesse fall, sprawling full length on his back.

Taylor kept firing. He drove a bullet into the fallen man, then another. Rhodes' voice reached him, calling his name again and again. Taylor fired once more, then lowered his rifle, he stared in astonishment at Jesse.

The Regulator was *still* alive, writhing on the earth. Jesse rocked forward, came to a kneeling position. He cried, 'I'll kill one of you sons of bitches before I die!' He turned his head slowly and saw his pistol lying two yards away, on the sand. Taylor caught the man in his sights once more. Jesse reached for the pistol, then pain hit him. He screamed. He toppled on to his side and lay kicking up sand and screaming. After a dozen kicks that stopped.

For a full minute after that, both

possemen sat, unmoving. Taylor found his arms were shaking quite violently. In his ears the silence, after the racket of guns, screeched like an ungreased axle. He thought, maybe it had finally happened. Maybe his nerves were finally shot.

Rhodes, gasping with pain, brought Taylor from his daze. He knelt over the wounded man, seeing blood all over the right leg and the sand around it. He asked, 'How is it?'

Through gritted teeth Rhodes said, 'Leg shot right through. Missed the bone, I think.'

The sheriff used a knife to cut away part of the cloth around Rhodes' wound, and used Jesse's bandanna to bind it. Rhodes glanced at the dead outlaw. 'He was a tough devil. Another one died hard.'

Taylor nodded. 'Maybe the meanest of the whole crew.'

'The Kid?'

'He never used to be like that, so easy on the shoot.'

Taylor was relieved to see Rhodes' wound was bleeding fast, but not spurting blood as it would if an artery was punctured. 'You handled the business better than I did.'

'Anyone can kill a man. Am I going to bleed to death?'

'Probably not. Keep loosening this tourniquet. There'll be help up here soon.'

'What about you? Are you going after them?'

'Uh-huh.'

'What'll it do to you, if you have to kill Paco?'

Taylor thought a minute before answering. 'I hope to God it doesn't come to that. Way I see it, I'm the best chance of keeping Paco alive. Whatever happens, I think Pilar and me are all washed up. She called it right. She didn't like what I turned into; maybe I don't either.'

'Get rid of that badge then.'

'Too late, now. This has to get finished.' The lawman stood. 'That bandage should hold you 'til help comes.'

'Taylor?'

'What?'

'We talked before . . . about the Kid's legend. And it's a lot bigger now.'

'Well?'

'Bring him back alive. Bring him back and hang him. They don't make legends out of those who die like common criminals, on the gallows. You put a bullet in him and he'll be a hero. A martyr. The Robin Hood of the South-west, the wronged youth — '

Taylor smiled bitterly. 'Culwhatshis-name, the sun God?'

'Give him the due process of the law and he'll be dead, forgotten. Shoot him and he'll never die.'

Taylor mounted his horse. He said, 'He may not give me any choice.' He kicked his horse in the ribs and rode away from Dead Man's Wells.

14

The ambush at the Wells had driven the Regulators off course; from heading west they now veered south. Back into the fringes of the White Sands.

By noon they had to stop. They fell from their saddles in the lee of great dunes that humped against the sky. Each man had but a few mouthfuls of water left in their canteens. They gave their horses a little and drank a very little themselves, rolling the water in their mouths before swallowing. Paco lay in the meagre shade his horse gave. He thought about the water they'd left behind them at Dead Man's Wells. In reality, it would have been a brackish pool, green and harsh with alkali, but in his imagination it was a mountain rivulet, flowing downslope, sharp on the tongue, with the taste of ice in it. He sucked a pebble and dreamed of that chill, clear water playing over stones . . .

The Kid had crawled up the flank of the nearest dune and lay just below the crest of it, where he could see beyond. He said, 'You're a good kid, Paco. You're the last one left with me, after all the rest of 'em . . . '

From the tone of his voice, you'd think the other Regulators had run off and left him! Paco said, 'All the rest of 'em are dead.'

'You thinking about your mama? You should have thought about that before you came along with us. Taylor's got taste, I'll say that for him. Your mama — I wouldn't mind myself . . . ' He grinned at the look Paco gave him. 'No offence. Pilar's a good-looking woman, that's all!' Paco scowled and the Kid laughed. 'Don't take on so, kid! I'm just speculating!'

They lay in silence once more. Gazing at the Kid, Paco felt a strange feeling ease over him, a peculiar coldness formed in his stomach. After a time, he found the moisture in his mouth to ask, 'You figure they killed Jesse?'

Nino took another long, searching look at the country ahead before replying. 'I figure. Funny thing. I've always had an instinct. Riding up to the Wells there, I *knew* something wasn't right. I had a feeling we'd run into guns. Good thing I rode back to you for that chaw of tobacco, otherwise I'd be where Jesse is. Right now he's frying hotter than even we are!'

The Kid laughed again; it was a laugh cracked with thirst. For the first time Paco thought he heard strain, a little craziness, in that laugh.

Paco said, 'You could have warned him . . .'

'Jesse should have watched out for himself. He was like me, once. Had the same instincts. Only back at the Wells, he forgot them. You only need to forget once.'

'And now he's dead.'

The Kid said, '*Que lastima!*' (What a pity!)

'He was your friend.'

The Kid glowered at Paco a second; then he continued laughing.

Paco's arms and legs began to tremble slightly, suddenly he realized what the coldness inside him meant. He was afraid. He was afraid of the Kid.

Paco thought, I don't want to die out here, in this awful place where only outlaws would come to hide. Why had he done this, come along with these Regulators, these men marked for death? Just to spite Taylor, to get his own back on his mother? Because Taylor had killed Quirino and taken Vincente prisoner? Aloud, he asked himself, 'Why, Paco?'

The talking to himself disturbed Paco, maybe he was going crazy. He stood, swayed a little. The pebble was still on his tongue, which felt thick, sore and swollen in his burning mouth. Time had slipped by him; perhaps he'd dozed. The sun hung, a blazing silver gong, halfway between noon and dusk. He saw sweat, thick and rank and white, had fouled what had once been his best shirt, the cloth was heavy with it. Taylor had said he looked quite a gentleman in this outfit . . .

The strange world of the White Sands moved before him, a salt-white lake, the surrounding dunes wavering in haze, like weird cones of snow in this great heat. Taylor had said . . . what had he said? Something like: *That's how I'd treat a kid and you ain't one no more. I'm trying to keep you alive, Paco . . .*

The Kid came towards him, leading his horse. He said, 'Let's go.'

Paco blinked to get sun spots out of his eyes. 'Where?'

Nino didn't answer. He walked south-west and Paco followed.

They came to the edge of the White Sands. The land before them was no paradise — a bare, stony desert rising gradually towards the mountains, but at least the sands were behind them.

165

Paco walked in silence, but it seemed the Kid couldn't stop talking. He said, 'If it wasn't for Taylor . . . before he came along, we wouldn't have ended up like that, hiding out in that kind of country. The law was something you scared off . . . or bought off. They rode around *us*. But Taylor . . . ' After a moment, the Kid asked, 'You thinking about Pat O'Keefe?'

'I never said — '

The Kid halted; he yanked on the reins so violently his horse half-reared. 'Goddamn you, Paco, I told you! I never meant to kill Pat!'

Paco turned and saw the Kid's face was red with anger. His eyes were wild and bloodshot, his lips were blistered and there was salt in the faint stubble of his top lip and chin. The Kid lifted his voice. 'Why'd you keep saying that?'

The Kid's hand was near the grip of his pistol and he was trembling. Fear tied a hard knot in Paco's belly. He swallowed a wedge of it in his throat. 'All right, Kid.'

For a moment Nino stared. The peculiar thing was, it didn't seem to be Paco he was staring at, but something beyond him. Then they began walking again. Almost to himself, Nino said, 'Yes sir, Taylor. Well, he warned me . . . I should've killed him then, when I had the chance. I wonder why I didn't? If anybody'll get me, it'll be him.'

Paco tried not to listen to the Kid talking, talking, he was growing weary of it; now he looked up, startled. 'Nobody's going to get you. That's what you always say.'

Nino grinned. It was a lopsided grin, as wild as his eyes. 'That's right! That's what I always say! It's just that Taylor . . . Taylor's too like me. He knows how I think. He'd make a good outlaw himself. Knows lots of tricks . . . old Apache tricks. Even squawed with 'em. Didn't it bother your mama, sharing her bed with a man that'd lain with squaws? Wasn't she particular?'

Now it was Paco's turn to halt. He glared at the other man. 'You want

167

to kill me, Kid, you'd better get it over with.'

'I don't want to kill you! Why'd you say that? That's crazy talk!'

'Sure.'

While Paco continued to glare, Nino lifted his canteen and drank. 'Nobody's going to kill you. Both of us are going to get out of this.' He passed the canteen to the other man. 'When we get to Mexico we'll have us some times. Tequila, women, good living! Set up a new gang and . . .'

Paco drank a mouthful. Shaking the container he judged they were almost out of water, there were perhaps two swallows left in the canteen. 'We might not get to Mexico. We might not even get off this desert.'

The Kid grinned. 'Sure we will. We're nearly at the mountains now. Good country from here on.'

'You reckon?'

'See that rise there? Good country past there.'

But the Kid was wrong. They reached

the rise and stared. The mountains were still at least fifteen miles distant, the front ranges wavering in haze. Before them wasn't the good country the Kid promised, before them was El Malpais.

A slight wind sifted dust over this primeval landscape. The Indians called it the 'land of fire' and it was the colour of fire. The desert was littered with broken rocks and shale that glittered with sunlight, and then the seared, rusty plain turned black, as a flood of jet-coloured rock poured in from the west, polished black rock that writhed and erupted against the earth in tortured convulsions.

Nino used his bandanna to wipe sweat from his face. 'We've come the wrong way. Out of the White Sands into this. We've swopped one hell-on-earth for another. The black rock — that's the meanest part. The lava beds. You never been here?'

Paco shook his head. 'Heard about this country. Never wanted to see it.'

'Well, we've got no choice. We have to keep going.'

'Why?'

'I know where we are now. There's a waterhole ahead, in those mountains. Ojo Caliente. Good water, too. But the straightest way to it is across the lava beds.'

The two men mounted their horses and entered the badlands. From all sides came waves of dizzying heat, trapped between rocks. Above, the pounding, coruscating sun. They came to the beginning of the lava, frozen waves of black surf that curled and whipped around ankles, razor-edged.

Paco said, 'We'll never get the horses across that.' He heard a note of despair in his voice.

'We've got to try.'

'It's like being in a furnace.'

'I'll take your word for it, as I ain't never been in one.'

Another mile and Paco's horse gashed its fetlock on a rock outcrop; it screamed and reared. Paco sprang clear, landed on his feet and his ankle turned under him. He fell, feeling pain spurt through his foot like hot liquid. He cried out. The horse came down awkwardly and he heard the snap of the off-front leg; the animal whinnied shrilly and fell, kicking out.

Paco sat up, kneading his ankle with both hands, swearing at his hurt. The horse screamed. The Kid said, 'Shoot that horse!'

'Shoot it?'

'Its leg's broke. Gooddamn you, Paco, you going to let that animal suffer?'

'All right — '

'Goddamn you, Paco!' The Kid pulled his pistol from his holster and fired. Both men watched the horse kick and die. 'God damn to hell any man who'll let a horse suffer like that.'

'I was just about to — '

'God damn you! God damn you and God damn Taylor! God damn the rest of 'em, they all run out on me!'

The Kid breathed heavily; he looked

171

suddenly weary, a defeated man. Paco began to speak and didn't. He was afraid once more; cold with fear, it was like the icy water he'd dreamed about, filling his belly.

There was a long silence while the Kid stared, fascinated, at the dead horse. Finally he asked, 'How're you?'

Paco stood, wincing, as he shifted his weight onto his injured leg. Nino asked, 'Can you walk?'

Paco managed four paces before pain halted him. He bent, clutching his ankle.

Nino scowled. 'We'll ride double.'

They tried that, the Kid riding in front of Paco. Half a mile along, Nino said, 'This horse is going to die under us.' He slid to the ground. Paco rode, the Kid walked. After another mile, they halted again and Paco dismounted, letting the horse blow. The Kid rested a hand on its trembling flanks, slick with foam. He mopped sweat from his red, blistered face and declared, 'There's no future in this.'

Paco, sitting, looked up at the tone of the other's voice. 'Leave me.'

'I can't run out on you, Paco.'

'Why not?'

'You're the only one stuck with me.' Nino shook his head. 'This is all because of Taylor. I thought he was my friend.'

'Leave me then.'

The Kid sat on the earth. He gazed at Paco strangely. 'No, we're going to Mexico! Set ourselves up down there . . . start over. It'll be just like it was . . . before Taylor put on that badge . . . it'll be all right, Paco.'

Paco remembered Taylor saying: '*You think you're the Kid's friend. He doesn't have any. Just people around him who get between him and the next bullet.*' Strangely enough, Jesse had said much the same thing. '*In case you get to thinking you and him are friends . . . the Kid always looks after himself.*' Jesse, dead now . . . Paco remembered how the Kid had smirked about that, about how his own instincts had held good when Jesse had got careless . . . got careless and got killed, and all the Kid — his so-called *friend* — did was laugh about it.

Paco stood. He climbed into the saddle. He glanced at the Kid. The older man looked pensive, turned in on his own thoughts. Maybe he was thinking, two men and one horse. There's no future in this.

Then the Kid smiled. It was a satisfied smile, as if he'd been wrestling with a problem and had now decided on a solution. He wiped off the sweat on his hands on his pants.

Paco said, 'Let's go.' He kicked the horse into motion. He glanced back. The Kid was standing. He'd produced the fringed gauntlets from his pocket and was pulling them on.

15

There were three parties converging on the same spot. This was Ojo Caliente, the Warm Springs, where an eye of clear water pooled in a sheltered place in the San Andres range.

From the south came three men on horseback — the Yerbys, Zeke and Mose, and their friend, Lem Scurlock. They were pale with dust, heads nodding with weariness, but they were still alert, their hands tensed around their weapons. Their appetite for revenge was still unsated.

From the north-east came Calvin Taylor, on foot. Almost as soon as he'd struck the badlands, his horse had picked up a stone bruise, so Taylor let the animal go. Few Anglos would have risked crossing the *malpais* on foot, but Taylor knew he was equal to it. He moved in and out of whatever shade and cover he could find, not hurrying. He was sucking a pebble and drinking only sparingly from his canteen, knowing he only had enough water to last him to the springs. He was thinking of the clear, never-failing water at Ojo Caliente, and of Pilar Garcia, and of Paco.

From the east came the Arizona Kid.

* * *

The Kid was talking to Paco. He was saying, 'It'll be all right, Paco. You'll see.' He was concentrating on the difficult task of putting one foot in front of another. There had been a horse, he remembered; what had happened to it? Had it gone lame, had he turned it loose, or had he just dreamed it ever existed?

He'd been walking all night; around him now was the pink light of the new day. His feet were aching and blistered, the sole of one boot had been ripped open by a razor-edged shard of lava, the same rock gashing his foot. He limped. His tongue was a bloated thing, blocking the fierce, dry place that was his throat; his head ached from the sun's pounding.

There was movement ahead of him. He squinted to see it clearly, but heat-haze and sunspots seemed to have invaded his vision, then cool air touched his face. He wrinkled his nostrils at a familiar stink. His senses were sharp as an animal's now, he identified that stench immediately: *water*.

He halted and stood swaying, trying to see. Gradually, the brightness in his eyes dimmed and he saw the gleam of water. It pooled in a cup in the rocks in the shadow of the mountains, with even a little colour, a miraculous green, at its edges. He found himself smiling a drunken, off-kilter smile. 'You see, Paco!' he said. 'I told you. Water!'

He managed a dozen staggering paces to the springs. Then he fell to his knees, toppling forward on to his face. His chin struck the earth, his mouth only inches from the water. His arm slipped ahead of him, splashing into the pool. He lifted a handful of water to his lips, drinking greedily, splashing some of the liquid on his red, sore face. He lay gasping. After a time he remembered Paco and wondered why the boy wasn't lying at his elbow, drinking also.

The Kid said, 'Hey, Paco — ' and began to turn his head.

A dim bulk stirred above him, a warning flickered far back in his brain. Instinct made him grab right-handedly for the pistol in his belt. Before he could reach it, something drove hard into the small of his back, ramming him forward. Another weight slammed against the back of his neck, grinding his lips, teeth and nose against the earth. His hand was still reaching for the pistol, then another something smashed against his fingers, numbing them.

He lay, pinned against the earth. A piece of very cold metal touched his ear.

The muzzle of a rifle; the same weapon came on cock. It was surprising how quickly that hard, chill sound jolted Nino out of his daze. His surroundings, which had writhed like smoke around him, came suddenly and cruelly into focus. There were two figures standing about, Zeke and Mose Yerby, plus the third behind him, pinning him down. The man standing above the Kid, his foot in the middle of Nino's back, identified himself by saying, 'You ain't much now, are you McCarthy?' Nino recognized Lem Scurlock's voice.

That only put more cold fear in the Kid's belly. Scurlock was an old enemy, a big friend of the late Sheriff Kelly, part of Kelly's gang.

Nino turned his head and glimpsed Scurlock. A tall man, thin as a skeleton, with shoulder-length dark hair, dark complexioned, moustached and bearded. He wore dark, shabby clothes and a wide-brimmed slouch hat. He seemed unusually well-armed, a full bandolier about his narrow chest.

He loomed over the Kid like some grim vulture.

Feeling returned to the Kid's right hand; pain surged through his fingers. Enough pain to bring sweat out on his forehead. He whimpered with his hurt.

Mose said, 'That's nothing, boy. That's only the start. We got a whole lot more of that laid up for you.'

Zeke nodded, grim-faced. 'We can't do no less. Not for Sam.'

Lem said, 'Zar Kelly too. You'll answer for that, you backshooter!'

The Kid yelled, 'Run for it, Paco! Get the hell out!'

He listened for running feet and heard nothing. A couple of those around him laughed; it was puzzled laughter. Lem Scurlock asked, 'Who's he yelling at?'

Zeke asked, 'Anybody back there, Lemuel?'

'Nobody. I can see for a mile and there ain't nobody.'

'Then he's gone crazy.'

The weight on the Kid's back eased and he sat up, crying at the pain in his hand. He saw his fingers were pulped and bloody. The hurt in them pulsed and swelled as if each digit might explode; he wondered if the bones were smashed. He saw blood on the butt of Lem's rifle. The Kid looked for Paco, wondering at Lem's words; he saw only open, empty desert.

★ ★ ★

Calvin Taylor saw buzzards turning in the sky. He made his way towards the spot they marked. It was perhaps a mile away, but it seemed the longest mile he'd ever travelled. He was so dizzy with the fear of what he might find he seemed to be walking on a carpet of air, inches above the black lava. The dread in him tasted like iron in his mouth.

The buzzards were on the ground, tearing at the carcass of a horse.

Taylor stared at the dead animal,

shaken by the relief that coursed through him.

Then he saw more carrion birds. They were spiralling down from the sky.

The same fear and dread came over him again. He wanted to stay where he was, rooted to this spot, but knew he couldn't. He began walking towards this new gathering of buzzards as if he was walking to meet his executioner. To himself, he said, please don't let it be Paco.

When he came upon them, the buzzards were down, scrabbling over something in the dust. When he identified what they were fighting over, a startling sound came from him: an animal cry of pain, grief and rage.

He started forward, swinging his rifle, and the buzzards rose, cawing, into the air.

A body lay there, twisted on its side.

The sheriff knelt by the boy and pressed a hand into his shoulder, shaking him. He cried, 'Paco! Paco!'

He sat a long time, saying, 'Paco' again and again, only this time barely whispering. If he said the name often enough, maybe he'd change this, put right what had happened. But nothing changed. The buzzards wheeled, screeching, in the air. The wind sawed away blearily as if mouthing an answer, but the words were muffled, Taylor couldn't hear them. The wind sifted sand into Paco's wounds, his face torn open by the carrion birds.

It seemed a long time before Taylor noticed that the back of Paco's *charro* jacket was dark with blood. There was a small hole in the centre of his back. There was no exit wound.

Taylor stood. He draped the body in his canvas jacket, remembering how like a *caballero* Paco had looked, the last time he'd seen him, outside the Oxford saloon. How like a man of whom his mother would have been proud. How handsome he'd been, before the buzzards got to his face with their beaks and claws . . .

Taylor wanted to do something to keep from thinking; he looked around for rocks to cover the body. He found just enough loose rubble to serve, although it hurt him piling them on the corpse. He stared at this grim pile for a long time.

Then he set off towards the west.

A hundred yards along he halted and stared back at the lonely grave on the black plain. It seemed such a pathetic marking. The rocks would keep buzzards at bay, but wolves and coyotes might still root up the body, given time. Taylor didn't doubt they'd be about their grim business once he was out of view. Taylor found he was shaking. Hot tears burned acid rills in his cheeks. They stung his eyes, already sore from glare. He was angry, most of all, at himself. He remembered Pilar saying; *'Five hundred dollars, Taylor . . . all you have to do is kill another Mexican'*. But it wasn't $500, it was $1,500 . . . if he stood here blaming himself, he'd go crazy, he wouldn't be able to function; he had to turn his anger outwards.

As he started moving again, walking westwards once more, he remembered the Kid saying: '*Maybe you ought to settle it right now while you have the chance . . . save us both a lot of grief*'.

To himself, Taylor said, 'You were right, Kid.' He clenched his fists with rage, the same anger a slow, insistent pulsing inside his skull. In his mind's eye he saw something that hadn't happened, the Kid before his gun, falling as the sheriff fired . . . in his head he heard the screaming of the buzzards as they rose into the air . . .

* * *

It was close to dusk when Taylor came to Ojo Caliente.

For the best part of a day he'd been travelling across a blasted and waterless land, sustained by only the last of his water and a few mouthfuls of jerky he'd allowed himself, supplemented by nuts, roots and bits of edible plant life he'd managed to scavenge. He was dazed with thirst and heat as he entered the canyon.

Not so dazed as to completely drop his guard, however, all travellers in this country came to waterholes eventually, so there might be enemies here.

He lay in cover at the mouth of the canyon, studying the ground before him for ten minutes or so, seeing nothing. He knew he ought to wait longer, but the thought of the water in the pool only a few hundred yards away was driving him crazy. He got to his feet and walked over to the spring.

There were tracks by the pool that were probably fresh, but he didn't care about that, not after he started drinking. All he could think about was getting water into his mouth and down his throat, splashing the stuff on his sore, blistered flesh . . . then he heard a boot toe kick a stone near at hand,

and pistols and rifles come on cock. He raised his head and saw he was in the centre of a triangle, with men at each corner. The Yerby brothers and a man he knew only vaguely, Lem Scurlock. Former buffalo hunter and hanger-out with the Kelly gang. And, by all accounts, a rough customer. They all had weapons in their hands, pointed at him.

Zeke smiled and asked, 'You looking for someone?'

Before the sheriff could find an answer, Zeke lifted his rifle. 'Get rid of your guns.'

Taylor thought about that, leaving himself defenceless before these men. The alternative was to fight. He would maybe get Zeke, perhaps another, and that would be it . . . then again, weak and slow as he was, they might riddle him before he could even get his hand to a weapon.

He decided he wanted to live, to get his revenge. To find and kill the Kid. He threw his Winchester and pistol on to the sand yards away.

Mose scooped them up. Zeke said, 'And your shellbelt. I figure you've got a knife hidden somewheres too.'

Taylor sighed. He handed over his cartridge belt and the knife hanging from a thong against his back.

Zeke was amused. 'You act like you don't trust us, Taylor.' He nodded to his brother. Mose and Lem strode off, vanishing behind a giant boulder.

Taylor managed to speak. In a cracked voice, he asked, 'I don't trust *you*? Why'd you take my guns? Why'd you hide like that? We're on the same side, Zeke.'

Zeke smiled. Lem and Mose reappeared. They were dragging a man between them. A dozen yards from Taylor, they halted and let their burden fall. The man twisted on his side, his knees tucked into his belly, his hands seemingly tied before him. It was the Arizona Kid.

Nino's mouth was gagged and his eyes were wild. His skin was red and peeling. Taylor stared at the captive, feeling a cold hatred rise through him, filling him from toe to crown. He began to tremble. A sound formed in his throat, a primordial grunt of hatred.

Mose leaned forward, and pulled down the gag around Nino's mouth.

The Kid screamed.

Taylor flinched at the sound of the scream knocking about between canyon walls. The Kid writhed against the earth. Taylor saw his hands were tied before him, and both hands were black, patched with the pink of scalded flesh, his fingers hinged, charred claws.

The Kid screamed some more, and then began to whimper. Mose said, 'We been working on him. Old Indian ways. Brother Zeke knows how. Start with his toes, then with his hands . . . all you need is a knife, some metal heated in a fire. We'll make him sing a long time before he's out of it.' He kicked the prisoner in the stomach. 'Sing loud enough, Brother

189

Sam'll hear you down there in hell.'

Scurlock nodded. 'And Kelly too. You ain't much of a gunhand now, are you, Kid?' There was a peculiar, lisping sibilance to his voice. He showed his teeth in a snarl; or rather the few brown and yellow fangs that remained in his mouth, which explained his lisp.

Mose grinned. 'Maybe Mr High-and-Mighty Law and Order here don't approve. Could be he's too chicken-gutted for this kind of thing. Lived with Apaches, squawed with 'em and all, but still got a white-man's stomach.'

Taylor said, 'The hell with law and order. You can kill him any way you like. Give me my gun and I'll do it.'

Zeke quirked an eyebrow. 'So much for the due process of law. You still thinking about O'Keefe?'

Taylor said, 'He killed Paco.' His voice caught as he spoke.

'Paco Garcia? That's too bad.' Zeke gazed at the prisoner. 'Now why'd you do that?'

Taylor stared at the Kid. He remembered how dark Paco's eyes had been, dark like his mother's, but it was the eyes the buzzards had taken first and the tongue. He said, 'Let me kill him!' His arms and his voice were shaking. 'Give me back my gun!'

Zeke scratched his trail beard. 'Can't do that, Taylor. See, there's something you sort of forgot to tell us. Remember back at Bad Water? When Brother Sam wanted to finish the Kid? What did you say to Sam? Something like: we're *all* going to share this reward? You was talking about five hundred dollars for the Kid, split between us. We risk our necks and get eighty dollars apiece. What you forgot to mention was there was *another* reward on the Kid. Fifteen hundred dollars' worth, and all for you.'

'Who told you that?'

'Don't try and lie about it, Taylor. We know.'

Scurlock had wandered off, now he returned, leading three horses to the waterhole. Catching the tail end of the conversation, he said, 'A sight ungenerous of you, Sheriff, forgetting to mention that. So we'll forget about you now. Split the fifteen hundred *three* ways. Not four.'

Mose said, 'If you was to put a bullet in the Kid, it'd be you who'd get that money. But why should you? It was us caught him.'

Zeke took a slow drink from his canteen, wiped his lips with the back of his arm. 'Things sure haven't worked out for you, have they, Taylor? Not since you pinned on that badge. You was after the fifteen hundred dollars and Paco got killed because of it. And O'Keefe and all the others. I suppose that puts your Mex woman out of the picture. The reward's just turned into blood money, Taylor; your blood.' He chuckled.

Mose said, 'Who cares about another dead greaser? That Paco, he was in on getting the Kid loose. Sam's dead because of him. That little spic

bastard — I'd've killed him myself!'
He smiled at the look Taylor gave
him. 'Why, Sheriff, you're looking like
maybe you want to see *me* dead. Well,
funny enough, that's how I feel about
you. So let's get to it.'

'Why? 'Cos of fifteen hundred dollars?'

Mose shook his head. 'Old scores to
settle.'

'Like you tried at Dirty Springs? You
yellow goddamn backshooter!'

'That accidental shot?' Mose nodded.
'Sure. But this time we finish it, face
to face.'

Scurlock made an impatient sound.
'Why don't we just put a bullet in him?
We can say the Kid done it.'

Zeke said, 'No. Mose is right. This
is a matter of family honour, now.'

Mose laid down his rifle. 'Yes sir
— family honour. We'll give him
his chance. Whenever you're ready,
Taylor.'

The sheriff asked, 'How you having
it, Mose? Guns, knives?'

Mose unbuckled his cartridge belt

and let it fall to the earth. A knife came into his hand — a double-edged stabbing knife with a vicious, foot-long spike of a blade. What was called an 'Arkansas Toothpick'. Taylor stared at this fearsome weapon, but Mose dropped that too. He lifted his great hands, the thick, furred fingers wide-spread. He braced himself like a wrestler. 'Just stand up, face to face, like I said. I aim to kill you with my bare hands.'

16

Zeke settled himself on a rock, his rifle laid across his arms. If he had any anxieties for his brother, he didn't show them. Lem also cradled a rifle in his arms and had a pistol in the cross-draw holster on his left hip. The Kid sat, hunched over his crippled hands, gasping and swallowing against his pain.

Taylor remembered Paco again and felt an ache of hurting and grief. But he'd better stop thinking about that quick, and think about here and now. If Mose killed him, Paco would never be avenged!

The sheriff took his time standing up. He hadn't eaten anything worth mentioning in twenty-four hours, which left him dizzy and tired, but at least he'd drunk a fair amount of water which might just keep him upright long enough to finish this. He couldn't match Mose's strength anyway, although he was taller than the other man, with a longer reach.

Lem said, 'I seen Mose kill a man with his hands once. Fair tore him apart.'

Which was probably lies, Taylor supposed; although studying Mose's shoulders — so powerful he seemed almost hunchbacked — the bull neck, the thick trunks of his arms, the spade-like hands with their scarred knuckles and long, spatulate fingers, it might just be true. Taylor remembered the fight around the campfire, those fingers clamping like bands of iron, and how quickly and easily Mose had moved, despite his bulk.

Mose took a step forward; instinctively, Taylor took a step in retreat. Lem laughed with contempt. He said, 'Like I was just — '

Taylor struck him in the throat with his elbow. Lem gagged and doubled over. Taylor flung himself backwards, striking against Lem and falling and rolling and coming up — with Lem's pistol in his hand.

Zeke got to his feet, lifting his rifle. Taylor flung himself backwards once more, struck on his shoulders and rolled under a horse's belly, so the animal was between him and his enemies. Zeke lunged forward, bringing his rifle to his shoulder. Taylor drew a quick aim from the ground and fired. Zeke stumbled, he half-somersaulted headlong. Taylor scrambled to his feet. There was a shot fired at him, the horse screamed and reared. He drove a bullet at the muzzle-flame, then turned and ran for the canyon mouth. He began to zigzag as he ran, Apache style. Two shots came after him, then he felt the breath of another bullet, but he wasn't hit.

★ ★ ★

Zeke sat up, one hand pressed to his right side. There was blood all over his shirt front and his pants.

Mose cried, 'Zeke!'

197

It hurt like hell to breathe, but Zeke swallowed and said, 'I ain't gonna die! Get that son of a bitch!'

Lem said, 'He's only got a pistol and three bullets.'

'You want to leave that squaw-lover out there, where he can pick us off? Get him!'

'What about McCarthy here?'

Zeke gazed at the Kid and smiled. 'I'll take good care of him while you're about your business. Don't worry, there'll still be something for you to have fun with when you get back.' He stood, swaying. 'Run that bastard down, he's the one put this bullet in me.'

'Zeke — '

Some anger got in Zeke's voice. 'You're wasting time, boy!'

That decided the others; they mounted their horses. Mose said, 'This won't take long, brother,' spun his horse and galloped out of the canyon. Lem followed.

Nino said, 'God damn you, Yerby!'

Zeke nodded. 'His curse is on us all. Especially you. Why'd you kill the Garcia boy?'

Nino didn't answer that. Instead, he said, 'I hope Taylor's killed you.'

Zeke shrugged. 'Maybe he has. Maybe I've got my finish coming. But there's one thing for sure — you won't be there to see it when it happens.' He stepped past the prisoner, then halted, turning back. He brought his foot down slowly on the Kid's right hand, pressing the blackened fingers to the earth. The captive screamed, his face turning grey with shock. His eyes rolled back in his head and he flopped against the earth, seized by a trembling all over. When Zeke judged he was just about to faint, he lifted his foot and Nino lay, writhing. Zeke watched this for a little time, smiling. He began to hum a tune to himself, something he'd first heard down in Mexico, back in his scalp-hunting days. Then he moved over to the waterhole and, taking his knife, began to cut switches from the mesquite and other shrubs there.

He told the Kid, 'Maybe you don't remember: when you staggered in here, you was talking to Paco Garcia. Like Paco was walking alongside you. And all the time the Garcia boy was dead, and you'd killed him.' He could see the prisoner wasn't listening, he was in too much pain, but Zeke went on anyway. 'I guess you'd gone *loco* in the sun. Temporarily touched. Happened to me once.'

Zeke paused, listening for gunshots beyond the canyon. He trimmed the branches, humming some more. Once he paused when he drew in a sharp breath and pain took him. Zeke told the Kid, 'But I can see you're back in your right mind now. That's what's important. That you know what's happening to you. Wouldn't mean anything otherwise. We got to do this right. For Sam's sake.' He began to assemble the mesquite wands he'd cut in a small cairn before him; he was making what was called a 'squaw' fire.

17

Once out of the canyon, Taylor ran for cover. The mountain slopes were belted with mesquite and other low, twisted thorny trees, finding meagre purchases on steep inclines under the front range. He climbed these slopes until he found a flat place shouldering out of the mountain wall; he lay there, gasping.

It was nearly dusk, with only half an hour or so's shooting light left, but he didn't intend to strike out across the open desert where he could be ridden down. His only chance was to hide himself and let his enemies come to him, hope one of them would get within pistol range.

Taylor inspected Lem Scurlock's Colt. Lem hadn't kept it in good repair and the balance didn't feel right in his hand. It was a snub-nosed Peacemaker

.45, with the scroll-engravings on the short barrel mostly worn away, and a crack in the grip that cut into the palm of his hand. There were three bullets in the chamber.

Taylor scowled. Here he was, a hunted animal, run to ground in this desolation, with only three bullets between him and violent death. If he was still alive tomorrow, maybe he'd start growing up, get settled somewhere peaceful and live the life normal people lived, without guns or killing. Find a woman to settle down with, but not the one woman he wanted. Not Pilar . . . that relationship had blood on it now, and blood money. Fifteen hundred dollars of blood money. It was killed like Paco was killed.

The heat under the mesquites was thick and smothering; he was bone-tired; his body was battered and aching, but he couldn't take account of that. If he gave into weariness, he'd just sink into the earth and lie there until he was found and killed. He needed to find a final burst of strength if ever he was to get his revenge . . . even if he had to kill Scurlock and the Yerbys first. A tall order with just three bullets . . .

He used the tail of his shirt and his bandanna to clean the gun. It occurred to him that his enemies were slow coming after him . . . no sooner had he thought that when he heard the clatter of hooves and two horsebackers issued from the canyon. He heard Mose Yerby call something like, 'Tracks point this way!' The riders came towards him until he could identify their horses and colour of clothing: Mose and Lem. Had he killed Zeke?

Even though they must have known how poorly he was armed, the riders halted well beyond rifle range and stared upwards at the tangled vegetation above them. He heard a voice again, maybe Mose shouting instructions. Lem rode ahead and vanished from sight. Mose dismounted, his rifle in his hand, and stood, eyeing the slopes warily. Then he began to climb uphill, disappearing into the lower brush. The tactics were obvious: *they were going to get Taylor between them, close in on him from two sides at once*.

The lawman was pouring sweat. He mopped it from his face, then tied his bandanna across his temples. He began to shake with the fear that blocked his throat, the blood that pounded in his head. He tried to will that away, thinking of Paco and the revenge he was going to take.

Taylor moved further into cover, a bosky of mesquite and alamo trees behind a scatter of small boulders; a good lying-in-wait place, save that it backed too closely to the mountain wall, the crest of the front range looming steeply above him. He waited, lying on his face.

Silence grew dense in his ears. The first dusk shadows began to paint the slopes, which brought relief from the heat, but played tricky games with visibility. He could see no one; all he heard was the dry buzzing of a rattler's tail.

Then he heard a stone tumbling.

His ear told him that the stone had been dislodged off to the right and had clattered a long way downslope: *there was a man on the crest above him. Maybe Lem was up there already, but how far off was he?*

Taylor began to ease back. He glimpsed movement in the trees below him. Mose Yerby came into view, both hands to his rifle.

Mose paused at the foot of a bare slope and he glanced upwards. From the expression on his face, he didn't like the look of what he saw, but he set his mouth in a grim line and began to climb anyway. His feet churned shale and he slid back one step for every two.

Mose was coming into pistol range, in a minute Taylor could try a shot. With only three bullets, he'd better not miss. Taylor had almost forgotten Lem, above him somewhere. *If* he was still there. Maybe he'd moved off along the crest.

Mose swore as he slipped on shale. The voice in Taylor's head said, That's it, Mose. Keep coming. Just five more yards.

Mose climbed the five more yards. Taylor slid the barrel of Lem's Colt forward between clumps of cholla, resting the butt against the earth. He trained the front sight of the pistol on Mose's chest; he began to squeeze the trigger. He watched the hammer ear slowly back, listening for the dry click as the weapon cocked, thinking, keep coming, Mose . . . walk right into it . . . but the hammer didn't ear back far enough to cock. Instead it jammed, the whole mechanism stalled. Taylor strained on the trigger and nothing changed, except a cold wash of fear-sweat broke on his face and neck. He thought, God damn you, Lem Scurlock!

Mose kept climbing. He was getting so close, Taylor could almost hear him breathing, he could almost smell the sweat that darkened Mose's shirt. Once again, Taylor was going to have to tackle him hand to hand . . . those hands that could rend and tear a man like ripping a piece of cloth . . .

Mose halted, squinting, as he strained to see into the brush. And maybe he *did* see something because he jerked the butt of the rifle to his shoulder.

Suddenly there was a scream.

It came from the canyon, from the direction of the springs. Behind Mose. He turned towards the sound and Taylor sprang to his feet. He ran forward and leapt into space.

As Taylor plunged towards him, Mose lifted his rifle, his face startled; then Taylor struck against him. Mose was bowled from his feet; both men tumbled and rolled down the slope. Taylor fetched up in a jackknifed position, upside down and half covered in shale, which broke his fall. He crashed to his feet in this stuff as Mose reared to his knees. Mose had lost his rifle. As Taylor charged him he raised his fists. Taylor kicked him in the throat. Mose snapped over backwards like his neck was broken. But it wasn't, he rolled and came up with a knife in his hand — the Arkansas Toothpick. As Taylor lunged at him, he slashed out. Taylor felt fire along his right-side ribs, he yelled and spun away. He ploughed to his knees, one hand to his side.

Mose sprang, thrusting with the knife. Taylor flipped on to his back, he kicked out with both feet. They caught Mose under the ribs and lifted him into the air; he somersaulted forward, landed heavily, and rolled, smacking into the base of a cottonwood. He sprawled there, a long, curious sigh came from him.

Slowly, Taylor rose, swaying dizzily. Blood was running freely down his right leg from the gash in his side. He walked stiffly over to Mose's rifle, stooped and snatched it up, grunting with pain. He turned, working the lever, catching an aim on Mose's chest where he sprawled, winded, against the cottonwood trunk. Taylor heard the rattling of a stone skittering down the slope. He glanced up and saw Lem Scurlock framed against the sky, standing on the crest with his rifle to his shoulder.

Taylor dove forward as Lem fired.

Taylor struck the ground, rolled and fetched up on his back with the rifle to his shoulder. There was movement on the slope above him; he tracked it and fired. Lem pitched headlong. He rolled three times and came to his knees, lifting his rifle. Taylor shot him through the belly and then through the chest. Lem jerked to the bullets, lifting his rifle, trying to aim. Instead, he flung the weapon downslope, like a last defiant act. He toppled on to his face. Lem began to fall, slithering downslope in a little avalanche of rubble and loose stones, his descent slowing, then halting, as he ploughed into shale that buried his face and arms.

Taylor's own arms began to shake violently as he stared at the dead man. Then he remembered Mose and turned.

Mose had struggled to his knees, both his arms reaching behind him where the knife angled from his right side. He'd fallen on to his own weapon and striking against the tree trunk had driven it in almost to the hilt; the whole vicious length of the Arkansas Toothpick was inside him. He was already kneeling in a pool of his own blood.

Mose tugged at the knife; remarkably, he managed to pull it free. More blood came with that and Mose tried to scream, but the blood in his throat choked him. He swayed a moment, then toppled sideways and lay, kicking.

★ ★ ★

Once Zeke paused, hearing a crackle of shots beyond the canyon, then he smiled and carried on with his

210

fire-making, still humming the pretty Mexican tune.

He wrinkled his nose at the stench of burning flesh. He'd heated the barrel of an old single-shot gun, a relic he'd taken off an old Indian he'd scalped many years ago. When the barrel was glowing blue and purple he'd laid it against the soles of the Kid's feet. The captive still had some feeling left in his feet; it had been a good scream he'd let out. Now Zeke was going to find out if he had the same feeling left in his hands.

There was a length of metal turning blue and green in the squaw fire, the ramrod of the same antique gun. Zeke judged it was just about hot enough now. He moved over to the fire, drawing the metal from the fire with a pair of pliers. He paused to cough as he did this, tasting iron and blood in his mouth. The bullet in him was down under his left-side ribs. He was growing increasingly tired, seemed to be moving slowly, through water. Maybe his lungs were filling with blood. Perhaps the Kid was right: maybe Taylor had killed him. He was surprised to find he wasn't frightened by the prospect of death, if anything he was vaguely curious. It didn't matter, those gunshots meant that Mose and Lem had caught up with the lawman and paid him back, so Zeke wouldn't die unavenged . . . and he'd last long enough to finish the Kid, knowing Sam was avenged too.

Nino looked up from the earth, his face bloodless, his eyes barely focussing. At first Zeke had been afraid that Nino would die of shock, hearing him scream as the metal seared his flesh, but the Kid was tougher than he looked, he'd last a while yet. Which was a good thing, it meant he'd suffer more . . .

Zeke grinned down at the prisoner. 'Hold out your hands, boy!' His voice sounded thick and strange in his own ears. He lifted up the pliers so the Kid got a good look at the ramrod. 'You're going to hold this!'

The Kid tried to speak. After swallowing several times, he managed to croak, in a dry husk of a voice; he told Zeke to do something obscene to himself. Zeke laughed. 'You still got some guts left. But you're going to hold it, all right!'

The Kid stared at Zeke with hatred; then his gaze sharpened on something beyond. Zeke turned slowly; he heard Taylor call, 'Zeke!'

Zeke let the ramrod fall and grabbed his rifle. The ramrod fell across Nino's leg and he cried out. Zeke sank behind a boulder, though doubling over shot waves of pain through him, and pulled the rifle butt into his shoulder. He glimpsed Taylor at the mouth of the canyon, darting into cover. Zeke fired at him and missed.

Zeke began to cough again, blood came with his coughing. It was hard enough to keep his rifle raised, a weight of tiredness was crushing him and his eyes began to close . . . he struggled against that. He cried, 'Taylor! Where's Mose?'

The lawman's voice came from cover. 'Dead and gone to hell!'

To himself, Zeke said, 'Two brothers . . . two brothers!' With all the strength left in his voice, he called, 'Goddamn you, Taylor!' He tried to sight along the rifle, but dusk was coming, the world becoming dark. He was draining out like the day was draining out, but all he needed was the chance of one more shot . . . a clear shot at Taylor and the sheriff would join the Yerbys in hell.

Zeke heard movement behind him, the Kid stirring on the earth. Zeke ignored it, he focused all his efforts on spotting Taylor, on making that last good shot. Then Zeke felt sharp, hot pain in his back, under his right arm. This pain seared into him, sliding between his ribs. Zeke turned very slowly, catching in his nostrils the reek of burning flesh. The Kid was on his feet and the burning flesh was his hands, gripping the ramrod, the ramrod he was driving into Zeke's back. Zeke smiled to see the pain on the Kid's face, then folded to his knees and toppled on to his face. He stretched on the sand and died.

The Kid sat back; releasing the hot metal, he hissed and writhed in agony. Time passed, he didn't know how much time, then Taylor strode over, his rifle in his hand. He glanced at Zeke, six inches or so of the ramrod protruding out of his back; then his gaze moved to the Kid.

He asked, 'Why did you kill Paco?'

After a time, the Kid's pain eased. He managed to speak. 'I must've gone crazy. Crazy in the sun. I didn't know what I was doing.'

Taylor's face darkened. 'I figure you were down to one horse between the two of you. That's why you killed him. Everything else you did — maybe there was an excuse for it — but murdering Paco — ' Taylor's voice caught and he aimed the rifle at the Kid's face.

Nino bowed his head. He began to weep with pain. He said, 'Kill me!'

The Kid heard Taylor cock the rifle. The lawman said, 'You shot him in the back. Just like you and your gang backshot Zar Kelly. You never was nothing but a backshooter and a four-flusher. All the rest is just the stuff they write in dime novels.'

Nino waited for the shot. After a minute, he raised his head. 'Why don't you kill me?'

Taylor lowered his rifle. Some of the anger had gone from his face. 'I've changed my mind.'

'Why?'

'Something Rhodes told me about — there was a sun god, called Cul — something . . . '

'What are you talking about?'

'You ain't gonna end up like him. You're for the gallows.'

The Kid managed to sneer, 'You tried that before.'

'This time I'll get it done.'

The Kid put some pleading in his

216

voice. 'Anything but a hanging, Taylor. Turn me loose, even. How long do you think I'll last with these hands? I'd rather have a bullet.'

'Sure you would. That's why I ain't gonna oblige. Least I can do. For Paco . . . I'll have to tell Pilar about him, don't forget. I don't want any more Pacos wanting to be like you.' Taylor took Nino's arm and lifted him to his feet. He said, 'You don't get to be a hero if you die kicking on a rope.'

THE END

Other titles in the
Linford Western Library

THE CROOKED SHERIFF
John Dyson

Black Pete Bowen quit Texas with a burning hatred of men who try to take the law into their own hands. But he discovers that things aren't much different in the silver mountains of Arizona.

THEY'LL HANG BILLY
FOR SURE:
Larry & Stretch
Marshall Grover

Billy Reese, the West's most notorious desperado, was to stand trial. From all compass points came the curious and the greedy, the riff-raff of the frontier. Suddenly, a crazed killer was on the loose — but the Texas Trouble-Shooters were there, girding their loins for action.

RIDERS OF RIFLE RANGE
Wade Hamilton

Veterinarian Jeff Jones did not like open warfare — but it was there on Scrub Pine grass. When he diagnosed a sick bull on the Endicott ranch as having the contagious blackleg disease, he got involved in the warfare — whether he liked it or not!

BEAR PAW
Nevada Carter

Austin Dailey traded two cows to a pair of Indians for a bay horse, which subsequently disappeared. Tracks led to a secret hideout of fugitive Indians — and cattle thieves. Indians and stockmen co-operated against the rustlers. But it was Pale Woman who acted as interpreter between her people and the rangemen.

THE WEST WITCH
Lance Howard
Detective Quinton Hilcrest journeys west, seeking the Black Hood Bandits' lost fortune. Within hours of arriving in Hags Bend, he is fighting for his life, ensnared with a beautiful outcast the town claims is a witch! Can he save the young woman from the angry mob?

GUNS OF THE PONY EXPRESS
T. M. Dolan
Rich Zennor joined the Pony Express venture at the start, as second-in-command to tough Denning Hartman. But Zennor had the problems of Hartman believing that they had crossed trails in the past, and the fact that he was strongly attached to Hartman's Indian girl, Conchita.

BLACK JO OF THE PECOS
Jeff Blaine

Nobody knew where Black Josephine Callard came from or whither she returned. Deputy U.S. Marshal Frank Haggard would have to exercise all his cunning and ability to stay alive before he could defeat her highly successful gang and solve the mystery.

RIDE FOR YOUR LIFE
Johnny Mack Bride

They rode west, hoping for a new start. Then they met another broken-down casualty of war, and he had a plan that might deliver them from despair. But the only men who would attempt it would be the truly brave — or the desperate. They were both.

THE NIGHTHAWK
Charles Burnham

While John Baxter sat looking at the ruin that arsonists had made of his log house, a stranger rode into the yard. Baxter and Walt Showalter partnered up and re-built the house. But when it was dynamited, they struck back — and all hell broke loose.

MAVERICK PREACHER
M. Duggan

Clay Purnell was hopeful that his posting to Capra would be peaceable enough. However, on his very first day in town he rode into trouble. Although loath to use his .45, Clay found he had little choice — and his likeness to a notorious bank robber didn't help either!

SIXGUN SHOWDOWN
Art Flynn

After years as a lawman elsewhere, Dan Herrick returned to his old Arizona stamping ground to find that nesters were being driven from their homesteads by ruthless ranchers. Before putting away his gun once and for all, Dan forced a bloody and decisive showdown.

RIDE LIKE THE DEVIL!
Sam Gort

Ben Trunch arrived back on the Big T only to find that land-grabbing was in progress. He confronted Luke Fletcher, saloon-keeper and town boss, with what was happening, and was immediately forced to ride for his life. But he got the chance to put it all right in the end.

SLOW WOLF AND DAN FOX:
Larry & Stretch
Marshall Grover

The deck was stacked against an innocent man. Larry Valentine played detective, and his investigation propelled the Texas Trouble-Shooters into a gun-blazing fight to the finish.

BRANAGAN'S LAW
Alan Irwin

To Angus Flint, the valley was his domain and he didn't want any new settlers. But Texas Ranger Jim Branagan had other ideas. Could he put an end to Flint's tyranny for good?

THE DEVIL RODE A PINTO
Bret Rey

When a settler is cut to ribbons in a frenzied attack, Texas Ranger Sam Buck learns that the killer is Rufus Berry, known as The Devil. Sam stiffens his resolve to kill or capture Berry and break up his gang.